the teenage worrier's guide to Life

Also available by
Ros Asquith

I Was a Teenage Worrier

The Teenage Worrier's Guide to Lurve

The Teenage Worrier's Pocket Collection

*(includes The Teenage Worrier's Pocket Guides
to Romance, Families, Mind & Body and Success)*

Love, Fifteen

the teenage worrier's guide to Life

Written and Illustrated by
Ros Asquith as Letty Chubb

CORGI BOOKS

THE TEENAGE WORRIER'S GUIDE TO LIFE
A CORGI BOOK 9780552552820

13 15 17 19 20 18 16 14 12

First published in Great Britain by Corgi Books 1997
an imprint of Random House Children's Books

Corgi edition revised and reissued 2005

Papers used by Random House Children's Books are natural,
recyclable products made from wood grown in sustainable forests.
The manufacturing processes conform to the environmental
regulations of the country of origin.

Set in 12pt Sabon by
Falcon Oast Graphic Art

Corgi Books are published by
Random House Children's Books,
61–63 Uxbridge Road, London W5 5SA,
a division of The Random House Group Ltd,

Addresses for companies within the Random House Group Limited can be
found at: www.randomhouse.co.uk/offices.htm

The Random House Group Limited Reg. No. 954009
www.randomhouse.co.uk

A CIP catalogue record for this book
is available from the British Library

The Random House Group Limited supports The Forest
Stewardship Council (FSC), the leading international forest certification
organisation. All our titles that are printed on Greenpeace approved
FSC certified paper carry the FSC logo. Our paper procurement
policy can be found at www.rbooks.co.uk/environment

Printed and bound in Great Britain by
CPI Antony Rowe, Chippenham, Wiltshire

¡INSIDE!

Appearances, ART, ATTITUDE, Bottoms, Buskers, Campaigns, CATS, CLUBS, dance, DAYDREAMS, DEPRESSION, DIETS, ENVIRONMENT, EXAMS, fashion, FEELINGS, FUDGE, GAY, guilt, HABITS, HOMEWORK, IMAGE, JOBS, KISSING, Luxury, MONEY, MUSIC, Nuts, Omens, Parents, PARTIES, PHOBIAS, Religion, ROOMS, SEX, SKIN, Supermodels, TRAINERS, Vegetarians, and MORE...

Moi: travelling lite towards the Great Unknown . . .

Tear-stained pillow
Unmade bed
Cranny of cheerless roomlet
Apology-for-a-dwelling
Trivial town
Minuscule nation
Tragic Werld
Liliputian speck in Solar System
Paltry dot in Yuniverse
Cosmos
The Great Be Ond

Dear Teenage Worrier(s),
  *This volume, the – er – biggest and best El
Chubb extravaganza to date (chance-would-be-a-
fine-thing-I-should-be-so-lucky-and-other-assorted-
clichés) will encompass the Meaning of LIFE, the
True Nachur of Existence, the opposite of Banana,
Being and Nothingness Etck in all its myriad
diversity. As you may have noticed from my
address, above, I have not yet banished all traces
of Fear, Worry, Glume and Dume from my psyche.
I am certain, however, that, by sharing with you
(dear caring Reader) my innermost forebodings
and translating them into a rich and meaningful
tapestry, together we can conquer the werld and
make loads of dosh (I mean, improve the environment for future generations so that yumanity can
co-habit peacefully in this Earthly Paradise, Etck).*
  *Teenage Worriers looking for information on
how to embezzle, bonk and get free drugs would*

1

be better off dipping into MPs' memoirs or hanging around the House of Common behaviour. Similarly, fresh-faced Teenage Worriers hoping for a buke about gung-ho items like Gurl Guides or abseiling will feel only a brief frisson of disappointment at the brevity of the entries on these subjects – as they will instead be plunged into a Voyage of the Soul (ahem) that will make the Celestine Prophecy seem like Little Noddy.

Er, at least, that's my humble plan . . .

I have chosen as my, um, theme, more or less everything. We Teenage Worriers spend roughly 8 hours of each 24 in bed (OK, let's admit 14 hours for depressives, 3 hours for ravers), 7 hours at skule (we assume), leaving 9 hours in which to file nails, nail files, pick noses, yawn, dream how to make the 14 hours spent in bed – complete with snoring siblings, raging elders, putrefying socks – more exciting (I mean useful). Etck.

First, may I humbly thank you for the mountain of Lurve-mail in response to my previous humble tomes. These heartfelt missives, added to the sky-scrapers of old newspapers, DIY volumes and rem-nants of unfinished novel belonging to my Adored Father, have caused my Only Mother to consider moving out before she is engulfed by what was once, as she so reprovingly admonishes, a rainforest.

All of which has led me to scribble this on the backs of envelopes, junk mail, red telephone bills Etck in order to avoid More Guilt and, dare I say it? WORRY. For if writing my insignificant contributions to the mental health of the generation that will one day be ruling this Noble Planet is causing an eco-disaster, then should I be allowed to disturb the ether?

Sometimes I think that instead of being a nun I should become a Jayne. These are V. Religious Indian folk who wear masks so that they don't breathe in minute insects, and sweep the floor in front of them wherever they go so they do not tread on same. This also leads them to respect the lives of rats Etck who spread rather a lot of diseases and therefore help to kill rather a lot of Jaynes. Life is a hall of mirrors, they say, and it's all a question of balance.

What differentiates TEENAGE WORRIERS from other yuman inhabitants of Planet Earth (and places us in much the same camp as household pets, and with similarly varying degrees of charm and temper), is our lack of

a) Autonomy and
b) Finance.

For these we remain sullenly dependent on our parents (social workers, uncaring Irresponsible Adults, Etck), artificially tied to the bosom of the family (if we are lucky enough to have a family, lash, guilt, always someone worse off than you Etck) while our hormones are moaning 'Freeee me! Freeee me! Let me roam freeeee!' and the Child Within weeps 'Want a hot choccy!' Viz: Cause of most of conflict in home and much of conflict in

Word-at-Large (NB: Odd phrase that makes the planet sound like a criminal).

I V. Much hope the guide to LIFE will enable the average Teenage Worrier to find ways of making the 9 'Leisure' hours (plus weekends, holidays and the yawning abyss of the post-skule future) a profound and meaningful experience.

And now, forward to pastures new (ish)! Turn yourself from a dume-laden glume-maiden into a frolicsome filly flicking your fetlocks at the Yuniverse! (NB: Boyz turn into proud colts flaring nostrils and arching noble forelocks Etck). LIFE would be much easier, I often ponder, if whole Yuman Race was transformed into horses. That Jonathan Swift had the right idea when he wrote Gulliver's Travels and made the horses V. Noble and the people crazed ravening beasts intent only on guzzling, biffing and bonking. How I long for a more Spiritooal existence (ahem).

Lurve,

Letty Chubb

N.B. There are some helpline numbers at the v. back of this buke.

(xx)

HERE IS A BRIEF UPDATE ON MY LIFE . . .

UPDATE . . . MOI

SCARELET (interesting Freudian slip, must explore festering soul to uncover Hidden Agenda) – I mean, of course, SCARLETT JANE CHUBB or LETTY (it is NO fun being called Scarlett unless you look like flame-haired temptress crossed with vixen-from-hell).

I thought gurlz were supposed to stop growing at 15 or so, but it seems I am becoming more of a leaning tower of Pisa by the minute (whereas my little brother remains a bouncing sphere of Pizza). Those of you who are vertically challenged, however, should not feel envy, as I do not have the willowy grace of supermodel but more the aspect of a street lamp struck by a heavy goods vehicle from which citizens flee in terror of imminent collapse.

Hair still the colour of that bread that well-meaning middle-class mothers try to force down their infants when all the babas want is nice, pale, bouncy, ready-sliced foam. If my hair were only like rats' tails I wouldn't mind, but it is more like a Gorgon's wig with the texture of brambles. (Not that appearances are important to *moi*, merely vital.)

Good news: I think my nose has stopped growing. I haven't measured it for two days now but I *sense* a new stability . . . maybe I won't have to hire myself out as the Yuman Vacuum Cleaner after all.

Craters, spots and cold sores still chase each other like storm clouds over my mug, each battling for ascendancy according to ye passing seasons. The plukes are no respecters of the time of year, however, popping out and waving waxy tendrils whenever they spot a cleft-chinned wunderbabe approaching. Since the CCW is never looking at *moi* anyway, but always at my mate Hazel, this makes little difference to the well of loneliness I inhabit. (Cue banshees, violins.)

I am still planning to be a film director (having postponed my Spiritooal Desire to be a Nun and give up Sins of Flesh – not that I have, yet, tragickly had opportunity to experience said Sins) and have enrolled on a film course one evening a week, starting tomorrow. Who knows what great opportunities to meet V. Handsome – I mean V. Interllekshual – boyz, lie ahead!

I have completely relinquished my passion for Daniel Hope.

No.

I must be honest with you.

If I cannot be honest with you, then what hope is there for newshounds, teachers, lawyers, Werld Leaders to be honest? What hope for Werld Peace? Ecological Sanity? Future of our generation Etckh? Zzzzzzzzzzzzzzzzzzzzzz . . .

Sorry, dropped off to sleep for a minute. What I mean to say is, I do still carry a torch for D. Hope. I know I shouldn't. I know he's a rat who has abandoned me for two of my BEST FRENDZ. But that's how it is. Luckily, the torch is burning V. Low, sputtering, and could be snuffed out V. Kwick if someone tall, dark and handsome enough (I mean caring, sharing, and kind enough) came along to win my heart. Readers, if you have a spare brother out there, post him to me special delivery.

All right, I'll admit it. There is Someone Else in my life.

Or at least, in my Imagination.

And it just so happens that he is enrolled in the

film course too. That is NOT the reason I enrolled. As you know, I have always had ambitions to be a film director. But, well, it isn't entirely a coincidence. In fact my frend Aggy pointed him out to me. He has just moved into the neighbourhood. One of her zillions of brothers told Aggy he was going on the course. Ahem. The Cat is now out of the Bag. I would have enrolled anyway. Honest.

More about **Adam Stone** (swoooooooooon, hope his heart isn't like his surname Etck) later . . .

UPDATE . . . MOTHER
Alice Constance Gosling

My Mother is V.V. Anxious to give up her job at the kiddies' library. She complains of Falling Standards, is fed up that all the boyz want to do is take out Batman comcs, football annuals Etck and that all the gurlz want is V. Soppy romances about poor heroines called Sarah who get off with cleft-chinned hunks with polo-sticks, country houses, minions Etck. I say, in what way does that differ from an adults' library? Anyway, I saw her hiding a copy of *Passion among the Peonies* under her pillow only last week, so I reckon she is V. Two faced and snobby about this, though you would think a well-bred girl like her wld at least choose an author who could spell ponies right.

The lengths I have to go to to get attention
from my Only Mother . . .

She is, as ever, distraught about our Edukashun, believing (possibly rightly) that I have no chance of any of the magic A—C grades at Sluggs Comprehensive with its 'lively mix' of 85% free school dinners. Since Aggy is one of that 85% and also the cleverest Teenager in the Yuniverse, I feel somewhat ratty about these statistics and believe that they do not give a true and accurate version Etck of Real Werld. But Sluggs is desperately trying to beat league tables by expelling everyone in sight, cramming borderline pupils to get 'C' grades and abandoning all below.

Since I sadly cling to flimsy life-raft of middle-class values, held afloat by pushy parents Etck I'll probably scrape through, waving to less fortunate classmates drowning in rocky seas of discrimination, hurtling over cliffs of unemployment Etck just because they didn't get help with coursework or live in nice areas with lawns and roses round door Etck. Mind you, I wish I did.

Meanwhile my Only Mother weeps over Lost Opportunities like the poor student she forsook for the promising, young, angry, Romantick, Working Class Novelist who became my Father. The poor student, Neville, founded a komputer empire and now jets between his 6 houses, spending most of his time on a remote Caribbean Isle . . .

Another Deep Regret is that she abandoned her Art to raise her family. While I proudly support feminist values Etck I cannot help thinking my Only Mother might have been happier if she could

have put just a teensy bit of her Artistick
Temperament into ye simple values of Home-
making. Like occasionally cooking something
edible. Or ironing her children's T-shirts (just now
and then is all I ask). Or redecorating a room instead
of squandering her wages on oil paint. I am V. fed
up with the nursery rhyme freeze in my room now.

My Mother's latest Wild Ruse to get hold of
some dosh is to spend what little she has on a
komputer graphics course. She says this will enable
her to get jobz on Posh Magz. I don't like to tell
her that the staff of those magz are all about 12.
I am a bit Worried she may have an Ulterior
Motive for her course (like I do about mine, ahem)
and am keeping a Beady Eye on the Adult
Edukashun Institute just In Case . . .

UPDATE . . . FATHER
Leonard Anthony Chubb

My Adored Father still writes Do-It-Yourself articles
(based on his own tragick experiments in Home
Improvement), plays komputer games (invented by
Neville, the poor student my mother spurned, and
thus rubbing salt in Only Mother's wounds), and
writes about one page on his new novel a year . . .

His first (and only) novel, *Moving On*, which
made him Toast of London 22 years ago, has just

In Ye Chubb home.

been re-issued to a wild chorus of indifference.
We had champagne Etck on day of publication and
waited eagerly for cheques to pour through door. But
sadly not a single newspaper has reviewed it yet and
my Father has spent the last week storming round
bukeshops and demanding to know why they aren't
stocking his Great Work. Still, it's only 6 days since
the first copies came through so there is still HOPE.

Meanwhile, he languishes playing CITYSCAPE, in
which you have to build a city in space to house
yumanity after destruction of Planet Earth. New City
must have abundant ozone layer, acres of parks, zero
pollution Etck Etck. It is V. difficult, after you have
got all the eco-factors right, to house more than
about 200 people, so it is V. Elitist. But my Father is
always in V. Good mood if he gets to level 2, because
the komputer emits a cheering sound accompanied
by a host of little green figures with pink hair who
crowd on screen to award him with an encouraging
message re his virtues as a Saviour. The game has 48
levels, so he has long way to go. It will have to do
until he wins Booker Prize, gets a job Etck.

UPDATE... BROTHER 1
Ashley (18)

Interesting developments re Ashley for all those of
you who have written in begging to meet this wise,

witty, noble, handsome brother of mine. His posh fiancée, Caroline, has asked for a 'cooling off' period of 3 months to see if she really cares, they are too young to tie knot blah blah. Ashley is upset but, being perfect, is at Oxford knuckling down to his degree so that he can become werld famous brain surgeon to the Poor-and-Needy, though maybe by the time he qualifies he'll be required to lobotomize said Poor-and-Needy to prevent Revolution Etck.

My Adored Only Parents are more distraught because although Ashley V. Young to marry, fiancée's folks are loaded, so they were hoping for weekends away on yachts. And they complain about *our* generation being materialistic!

UPDATE... BROTHER 2
Benjy (5)

Benjy will be 6 soon, still has golden curls, eyes like forget-me-nots, cherubic mug, teeth like a piranha and a kick like a mule. He is still anguished about the floors. His latest obsession is that the mild pink bath mat is a disguised Martian that will abduct him if he is left alone in the loo.

I blame all these 'bukes that will feed his imagination' that my Mother keeps bringing back from the library. She then never has time to read them to him and he, being able only to decipher a handful

of words, finds his imagination somewhat overfed.
Kindly Big Sister then reads him the real story
which is, I admit, usually more frightening than
anything even he could dream up. He then goes to
bed in tears, only to wake and plague sister with
his company through rest of long night. How will I
get my GCSEs under this kind of pressure? It is
harrowing domestic circumstances like these that
examiners never take into account . . .

If I use the ravishing purple dye I bought to jazz
up my old T-shirt (having succumbed to an article
in *Smirk* saying purple was the Big New Colour) to
dye the bath mat, will it placate Benjy? Or will it
further convince him of the alien's chameleon
powers? It is such humble Worries that I hope to
address as I tread the weary pages of this work . . .

UPDATE . . . PETS
Rover, Horace and Kitty

Ah. **Rover.** My Solace among the woes of this
Weary Werld. My frend in need. Cat among Cats.
Rover has recently perfected her art of opening
fridge to the point where we now have to barricade
it at all times. My Father says it saves money,
as no one else uses it much any more. My cat
allergy is a trifle worse, but Lurve conquers all
and most of my spare money goes on flea potions

for Rover rather than allergy potions for *moi*.

Horace the gerbil is still revolting – I mean revolving – on wheel for eternity (I confess I am uncertain whether gerbils have souls), though Horace is not as bad as **Kitty**, my *bête noire* – or should I say *bête blanche*? Everybody (except *moi*) adores her, finding her playful kittenish ways (like when she pees in my bed or scratches my poster of Brad Pittbull) utterly charming. As a result, Rover is losing out on Lurve from the rest of the family, being old and on scrap heap of their fleeting loyalties. I have to make up for this, but it is no hardship. True Lurve always finds a way . . .

Kitty: appearance of seraph, temper of barracuda

Benjy: ditto for Kitty, previous page

UPDATE ... GRANDMOTHERS

Granny Chubb still shines like a beacon as the other great Lurve of my life. Also shines glasses, windows, as despite failing sight and arthritic joints cannot give up lifelong vocation as cleaner.

I visit her postage stamp of a council flat as often as poss and get all the Lurve, comfort, biscuits, hot choccy Etck that the rest of LIFE does not proffer. It is worth donning the tangerine and lilac bolero she knitted last month to do so. It is worth listening to stories of ye World War, Grandpa Chubb, how they lived for two weeks on half a biscuit and a slice of spam because she gave all the rations to my infant Father. In fact, it is V. Interesting and I mean to use G. Chubb as subject for my heart-warming-yet-cutting-edge film about how this once Grate Nation has spurned its old folk in pursuit of ye hollow grail of profit.

My **GCSE (Granny Chubb's Specs Endeavour)** fund is running rather low as result of my selfish escapades and I blush to think how my LIFE savings could have bought her a decent pair of spectacles. I fear she cannot decipher the sell-by date on the tinned cat food she so eagerly consumes and will succumb to food poisoning before I have saved enough. CAMPAIGN for Free specs for pensioners!!

Grandma Gosling, my mother's mother, is still what used to be called 'a lady' in that she treats a duke and a dustman just the same, ie: abusing both in a voice like a megaphone. She has never recovered from her belief that her Adored Daughter married (huh!) beneath her (a view sadly shared, I am beginning to believe, by my disloyal Mother) and that therefore her grandchildren are little better than oiks.

UPDATE...FRENDZ

Aggy is still my closest friend at skule. I have completely recovered from her brief sojourn with Daniel Hope. She was, as I expected, much too brainy for him . . . though it will be V. Interesting to see who conquers werld in later life: Blond, thin, handsome, articulate, well-connected, privately

**Beautiful Hazel and Brainy Aggy are still my
FAVOURITE FRENDZ**

educated, but – if I'm honest – only moderately
clever Daniel? Or Brilliant, shy, awkward, plump,
black, poor Aggy from Sluggs Comprehensive?
Send your predictions to L. Chubb and see if we
can prove my Father is wrong to say nothing has
improved since he was a lad (violins, moan,
sneaking suspicion he may be right . . .).

I am still V. Good frendz with **Hazel**, most-
glamorous-Teenager-in-Britain. As far as I know,
I am her only confidante – as she finds the gurlz at
the posh academy she now goes to V. snooty. Also,
if any of them knew she was going out with a gurl,
she is sure they wld burn her at stake, put slugs in
her tennis shoes Etck.

But my friendship with **Sarah Spiggott (Spiggy)**
is on rocks since she sped off with Daniel Hope in
her clutches. Yes, Reader, their Lurve still blossoms
(puke) and for some reason I no longer seem able
to consider Spiggy's groovy, loose-limbed Ozzie
flair as quite suiting my tastes . . .

UPDATE ... BOYFRENDZ

Brian Bolt

Those of you who have read too many romances about how the loyal quiet admirer finally wins the heroine's affections when her eyes have been opened to his charms by the feckless behaviour of the cleft-chinned wunderbabe she has hitherto fancied, may have been hoping that I started to return BB's affections. But, although his complexion has improved and he is V. Interested in Art, I wish he Lurved Aggy, rather than *moi*. Also, there was a further incident, whose constituents included custard and a pair of frogman's flippers, that I am too embarrassed to recount.

Daniel Hope

I can't wait for Spiggy (my one-time frend) to dump him for a surfer. When the salt tears flow from Daniel's sapphire eyes, causing his golden hair to curl in soft damp tendrils around his Noble Brow (phew, pant), I shall be the first to run to comfort him – I mean laugh scornfully, toss my proud mane and canter off into the arms of . . .

Adam Stone

The new object of my affections has shoulders a little too broad for perfection and hips just a mite narrow. His legs are longer than might perfectly suit you vertically challenged types. His eyes the

colour of midnight skies . . . his hair a dark bunch
of grapes . . . It is V. Diff for me to know what to
wear on the first evening of my film course. Must
look casual yet studious, bubbly yet sensitive.
Above all, creative. Will he notice *moi*? Sadly,
Benjy overheard me mulling this over with Aggy
and suggested I go dressed as Batman . . .

UPDATES . . . ECCENTRICITIES ETCK

I wish I could say I have managed to write the werd
that is about dying and rhymes with 'breath', but,
despite following my own excellent advice about
Trying Not to Worry, this continues to plague me.
I still say 'banana' instead. I wonder if I used a
different word, I might conquer this habit. Perhaps

'raincoat' would do it? Viz: 'The tragic news of her beloved's raincoat precipitated a storm of grief' or, 'Once he learned of his impending raincoat, all his hopes for the future were for ever dampened.'

No, I'll stick to banana for now, or else we'll all get confused. I still have a thing about even numbers, have to touch the floor twice if I drop something and am apt to pray loudly in stressful circumstances (I usually come to my senses if anyone appears and pretend I am rehearsing a religious play).

My fringe has grown and helps to disguise my nervous tic. I have managed to go out twice without my lucky rabbit's foot, although I admit I only got a few paces down the road on each occasion before retrieving it. Still, a small step for personkind . . .

NB: Before I start, I ought to point out another little eccentricity I have: I do not have a MOBILE. I think I may be last teenager in UK or even werld who does not (perlease write to me if you are in the same boat) but I must be honest and admit I have had two. My first was nicked by some rude boys and the second I left on the bus.

My adored parents have put their feet down on this one but I have now nearly saved enough for a pay-as-you-go, as life is a mere incomplete shadow of glume without a mobile . . .

And now, on with the buke →

CHAPTER ONE
AAAAAAAZE

*Tension is mounting re my first class on the film
course. I got V. Big Buke out of library which
turned out to be published before WW2 and
showed ancient cameras with spools the size of
tractor wheels and V. intricate sprockets, flanges,
twinges, widgets, spridgets Etck. Not surprising
they started off making silent movies or soundtrack
would have been full of sounds of cursing, heaving,
springs breaking, ligaments twanging, actors
shouting to make themselves heard above din Etck.*

   *500 pages on the development of 'talkies'
and the future of colour film, though doubtless
fascinating in their way, induced alternating panic
attacks and prolonged bouts of snoozing. Where
was the key that would unlock the door to the
glamorous werld of Hollywood . . . ahem, I mean
the serious, artistic, heartfelt side, of course?*

   *Wondered briefly if I might make a splash by
reinventing wheel and making V. Grainy black-and-
white silent movie with lots of stills for cheapness –
I mean atmosphere. Cld make powerful impression
on Adam Stone, sorry, tutors, for street cred, commit-
ment, the simple dramatic image that Says All.*

Carted vast tome back to library and asked if they had biog of Tarantino, but was taken to sports section by helpful but aged librarian, clearly under impression Quentin was a striker for Inter Milan and delighted by joys of Gurlz entering realms of Boyz Etck. Confusion sorted just in time to find V. Sultry Gurl with exposed navel in front of moi taking out entire library's contemporary film section (three bukes). Begged her to let me have just one.

'But I need it for my course,' she murmured in husky Californian tones. (I mean by this not that she is a Californian husky, but that . . . well, you know . . .) Gaaaad!

'Er, would that be the, um, New Directions course, starting Thursday week?' squeaked moi, still hypnotized by navel, which appeared to be winking dismissively at Yrs Truely Pathetick. She undulated her neck in a manner that made her head approach the affirmative and glided out, the vast bukes seemingly weightless in her slender yet forceful grip.

Arg! Competition so early in the game!

Raked rest of library and found Adventures of the Silver Screen (pub. 1956), How a Film is Made (pub. 1954) and Let's go to the Cinema – all in the kiddies' section. Pretended to the librarian they were for small sibling. Got rather involved in Let's Go to the Cinema, in which a V. shy 10-year-old gurl, who lives on a V. remote Highland Island and has never seen a film, swims treacherous loch in midwinter, seething with murderous undercurrents, German submarines, flocks of Nessies, tidal waves

*of yuman waste Etck (I hv made up some of these
bits to heighten drama) to fetch doctor for sick aunt.*

*Her prize is a visit to the cinema, her first taste of
the Silver Screen (popcorn also), her first vision of a
werld beyond her island home, blah blah. This
seemed a pretty stinky sort of prize for such acts of
selfless heroineism, but just the same was wiping
tears from nose when realized I was hurtling through
unknown territory having got on wrong bus.*

*Had to get two buses home. Arrived to find
supper burnt to crisp in oven. Berated Only
Mother who announced she was not a slave, why
didn't I make supper for her now and then Etck.
Why do Adults always start discussion on Meaning
of Life when you want something simple like a fish
finger that doesn't look like an old firework?*

*Cried self to sleep over Highland gurl. Woken by
Benjy in throes of nightmare re bath mat. It had
taken him to Mars, planet of free Mars bars, then
betrayed him by thrusting him in vat of boiling
chocolate and threatening to pull Horace's
whiskers out. Parents as usual sleep through
Benjy's howls with devastating indifference. Took
him to check Horace's whiskers. Had to count
them twice, infuriating sleeping Horace who bit
Benjy in revenge, thus increasing Betrayal Factor
and size of tidal wave pouring over moi from
direction of Ickle Bro's peepers.*

*Tucked him up in bed. Turned out lights. Turned
off Father's komputer. He was sprawled asleep in
front of it at crucial moment in CITYSCAPE.*

Knocked half-empty lager can into Only Father's lap by accident. He merely groped damp trouser region smiling and muttering 'time, gentlemen, please', clearly a throwback to earlier era of sensible licensing laws.

Returned to bed pondering Byooty Sleep, Nachur of Yuniverse, hairdo of Adam Stone, identity of Navel Gurl in Library Etck. Asleep at dawn.

Must comfort self with prospect of this Alphabet creating zillions of sales worldwide. I begin, as before, with the AAAAAAze ...

ABSEILING

A-A-Aaaaaaaa

If you think El Chubb is ever going to be seen dead Abseiling you have an *autre* think coming, *mon amie*, and anyway if she were to pursue this seriously Luny activity dead is what she undoubtedly would be, and serve her right too. Why, I ask you, dear Student of LettyLIFE, did the great Creator of the Werld, the Yuniverse Etck invent gravity and bad eyesight to keep us stuck on the surface of the planet and imagining the globe is nice and flat if all we do is swing about in the air instead? Outward bound types may find it sweeps cobwebs Etck from Slough of Despond. Personally, I think if this happens it's only because Abseiling makes you realize there are

more frightening things in LIFE than Spots, Flat
Chests, Mad Parents Etck, to whit, staring Banana
in the face while swinging on the end of a piece of
string. Abseiling Lunies allegedly stave off this
Certain Fate by investing in lots of safety harnesses,
helmets, padding, LIFE insurance (not really) Etck.

ABYSS

The Pit of Despond into which you fall when your
LIFE Plans backfire, eg: Lurve Object telephones
three minutes late, Gerbil shreds only pair of leg-
gings, Wig falls out after bleaching, Etck. This first
is worst and is the longest three minutes known to
Yumanity, but is better than your Lurve Object
never phoning at all, as happens to *moi*.

See also DEPRESSION, FEELINGS,
PSYCHIATRISTS.

ADVERTISING

Adored Mother and Father sometimes go on as if
Advertising only started having its Wicked Way with
us all from about the 1960s, when window-cleaners-
turned-fashion-photographers started manipulating
our Dreamz with pix of Gurlz-Next-Door who

happened to look like Supermodels, and sneaky psychology began to replace the old corny stuff of actors looking like ventriloquists' dummies holding up products that nobody in their right minds would believe in.

But I have seen in Old Bukes that Advertising has used all manner of scams to make you believe LIFE is meaningless without some vital Stuff or other *for decades*. In the 19th century, con men in top hats were always getting people to believe they had the Elixir of LIFE in a bottle. After all, it only takes advantage of a Yuman quality that Yr Favourite Tomes, namely those by El Chubb, are always on about – ie: WORRYING. Biggest Worry of all, of course, is Banana. Advertisers don't quite tell you they can get rid of that, but they do say they can make Yr LIFE so wonderful in the meantime that when you do finally get there, you will Know that you lived LIFE to the full, thanks to Gluggo Drain Cleaner Etck.

Advertisers defend their often dodgy practices, bending of The Truth Etck by saying it makes people buy more and therefore creates jobs, stimulates Economy Etck. I reckon the only Good Thing to be said about Advertising is that if you get to work in it yrself they pay Qu. Good Dosh. Then, of course, *you* have to learn all those speeches about how it creates Jobz, stimulates Etck Etck . . .

ALADDIN

Many a time I have burnt midnight oil in attempts to make lamp that will grant everyone all of their LIFE's wishes – ideas on a postcard please. I wld certainly like to have a genie I cld call up at any time of the day or night, who would make my every wish Come True. (Unfortunately I think even if you have a V. Handsome Genie you are not allowed to get it to fulfil Yr Every Wish personally, as it were,

Even a V. Handsome
Genie might not
fulfil Yr Every Wish . . .

because it is of the Spirit Werld, shame, whinge
Etck.) Sadly, the only genie I have met is my
Mother's boss at the library, Jeanie Stropp, whose
name doesn't enable her to do anything magical
except send out fines to single parents on income
support so fast they've hardly had time to get the
books home in the first place. Maybe this is how
Aladdin's genie got his original treasure together.

ALPHABET

Why not make one for your little sibling? Or for
your worst enemy? A is for Agony, B is for Blisters,
C is for Cyanide, D is for Dume, E is for Ennui . . .

ANIMALS

Many Teenage Worriers are concerned about
Animal Rights and certainly if you look at how
chickens Etck are treated in today's hi-tech farms
you feel V. Sick. It is hard to imagine that the
Food chain, delicate balance of Nachur Etck is
not being seriously disturbed by the imprisoning,
injecting and dodgy feeding of our Animals and
since campaigning for their rights to a decent
LIFE also makes us have a better chance of same,

**If you don't want eggs from battery hens,
check they are 'Free Range'**

it seems a V. Sane thing to L. Chubb. It is well
worth finding out more about this and joining an
ecological group as there is V. Little you can do
about Animal Rights on your own.

Respecting your pet(s) is one thing you can do
and, as someone with an allergy to cats who still
has one on her bed most nights, I know what I'm
talking about. NB: If you are allergic, though,
don't get a pet. My folks would not have got me
Rover if they had known. It really isn't V. Good for
you. Remember the old saying: 'A pet is not just
for Christmas, it is for LIFE.' And certainly that
cute ickle ball of wool may not seem such fun
when it is a vast panting hound demanding walkies
every two hours and half a cow for breakfast.
THINK B4 you get a pet, whether you really want
to look after it, rain or shine. If you DO, it will
reward you with Lurve.

See CATS, DOGS, GERBILS, HORSES, PETS.

ANTHROPOLOGY

This is a V. Fantastic thing for Teenage Worriers
to study as it helps you understand Nachur of
Yumanity. Why do we need lightbulbs, toothpaste,
fishcakes Etck when we could be communing with
Grate Unknown from Hammock Etck? It takes
you away from yr own obsessions with spots Etck
and on to a wider canvas which shows you that
it's possible to be unhappy (I mean happy) in a
thousand different ways.

Imagine, for a moment, the incredibly different
LIVES led in Four Corners of Globe by other kinds
of people: nomads like the Bedouin, who still travel
by camel and are respected not for possessions, but
for 'Reputation', ie: nice attributes like honesty,
kindness Etck which our society seems to undervalue

in El Chubb's humble opinion. Or how about the Wayapi, the Amazonian People who have been hunting in the Amazon Forests for 5 centuries?

Then there are Aborigines, right on the doorstep of White European culture, who are the indignant (I mean indigenous) peoples of Australia. When I was best frendz with Sarah Spiggott before she took Daniel from me, she told me a lot about them and about how they, like the Native Americans before them, are being hounded off their lands and 'Westernized' Etck. Why anyone shld think people wld prefer to live in high-rise slabs of concrete rather than roaming deserts, mountains Etck with their mates is a mystery to *moi*.

A V.V. old Aboriginal artist, Emily Kngwarreye, who died in 1996, did not see any white people until she was 9 years old. She started painting in her 70s and became V. Rich and Famous, exhibited all over the werld and earnt vast amounts of dosh but continued to live in traditional hut. Maybe there is a LIFE lesson here . . .

APOLOGIES

One of the scariest things I ever heard is that the first French word that Hitler's troops learnt when they were invading France was '*Pardon*', which is French for 'Sorry'. This is an instance of how the spirit of the Apology can be abused, but unfortunately there

You can take apologies too far . . .

are many much less serious but still disturbing egs
than that of how people say 'sorry' as a habit when
they don't really mean any such thing. Those big,
shambling blokes who look like yaks and push you
out of the way to get on the bus sometimes say it (if
they notice you're there at all); so do V. Busy
Looking people with suits and mobile phones who
crash into you and say it having realized only that
something soft and squeaking might have scratched
their polished elk-skin briefcase in the course of
hurtling off it into the path of a speeding truck.

It is clear, however, that if you hope to avoid
some of LIFE's pitfalls then it is a good idea to know
how to Apologize gracefully, and that an Apology
genuinely offered is one of the most attractive and
disarming qualities a person can have. Actions,
however, have to be more important than werds,
or Apologies are nothing more than luke-warm air.

APPEARANCES

Do not judge by Appearances, you can't tell a buke by its cover, handsome is as handsome does Etck. Sadly, these fine phrases are not V. Comforting to your average puny, speckly, suppurating Teenage Worrier. Of course I wld *like* to subscribe to the Belief that the Soul Shines through even the cloudiest exterior and that I am Lurved for myself alone and not for mere Outward Appearances . . .

I blame the Teen Magazines like *True Luv, Smirk, Yoo-Hoo!* and the new, best-selling, excruciating *Peteet* for making us Gurlz wish we were spindly giantesses with floorless complexions, eyes like planets and teeth like a double row of keyboards. And now we're supposed to bake our own bread, run for parliament and have a couple of designer kiddies too.

Smirk would say: 'Find a style that suits you and stick to it.' The next week the same writer would tell you to 'Experiment with a wide variety of styles,

don't be shy.' With advice like this, no wonder
Teenage Worriers are confused.

L. *Chubb* would say, 'Don't concentrate on your
weak points. If you don't mention them, no one
else will notice.' Eg: A V. Nice gurl at school told
me how miserable her nose made her recently and
ever since it has made me miserable too, as I can't
stop noticing it. I never did before.
CONFIDENCE TIP:
Banish pix of Naomi Campbell Etck from your
poster collection and instead go for V. Interesting
women like Virginia Woolf, Grandma Moses,
Germaine Greer Etck. This will have added value
of making you look V. Intelligent as well as, um,
good looking by comparison (not that we care
what people think, do we? Cough, splutter).

See also FASHION, IMAGE.

ARCHITECTURE

HRH Prince Charles, Hair to the Throne (does his
bald patch mean his chances of becoming King
are diminishing further?), often goes on about how
terrible Architecture is today, how arrogantly
Architects design things that look like giant cheese-
graters, milk bottles Etck for people to live and work
in, without caring about the nice old crumbling,
pigeon-infested buildings standing around them.

El Chubb, Heroine of 21st Century City Renewal Etck and killer *CITYSCAPE* champione, wld qu. like to consider Architecture as a poss. career if the impossible happens and Hollywood stardom does not pan out. It seems to *moi* that it is a role in LIFE that can considerably cheer up the Yuman Race as they go about their daily grind, and Better Housing in particular is something that wld help lift the mood of many people currently inhabiting V. Depressing places built out of slabs of stained concrete Etck.

But it is not just a matter of the right Architects, but the right Attitude too. A few V. Flash Architects can get stacks of dosh for buildings hardly anybody uses, while councils Etck have to build estates on budgets which mean the tenants practically have to make their own bricks. There is something Wrong here surely, and if you care about this Ishoo, you cld:

a) Study to become an Architect yrself and try to help.

b) Submit proposals to the Teenage Think Tank for renewal of Urban Living Etck.

ART

Art is usually thought of as a V. Posh thing that yr parents Etck pretend to be interested in, celebrations of the highest manifestations of the Yuman Spirit

Etck, but for this reason Art that is being made by new Artists sometimes isn't recognized as Art at all. Some Artists today try to undermine V. Respectable Art by making sculptures out of wet T-shirts with oranges inside, dead fish, or lavatory bowls exhibited in posh galleries Etck. I must say I sympathize with this Attitude, and so does Benjy, who prob enjoys this kind of Art more than any other.

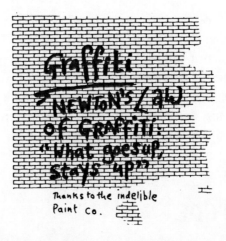

Graffiti
NEWTON'S Law
OF GRAFFITI:
"What goes up,
stays "up""

Thanks to the indelible Paint Co.

El Chubb nevertheless recommends escaping LIFE's trauma by immersing self in Art as often as poss, appreciating great pix Etck. It is not a matter of just going 'wow, wicked' Etck at Posh Art you have been told it's OK to like even though you don't understand why, but of twigging how some of the cleverest people at recreating LIFE on canvas, in bukes Etck, saw Lurve, Hate, War, Peace, Washing-Up, Plukes Etck, hundreds of years ago.

It can be V. Humbling and Enlightening because it helps you to realize people have felt just like you lots of times before.

See also HOBBIES.

ASSERTIVENESS TRAINING

V. Imp to be Assertive in today's Cut-and-Cut Werld where the Haves have lots and the Have-Nots have not. But take it easy: first, learn to spell werd 'boo', then gently practise it in front of mirror before trying it out on new-hatched chicks, progressing through sparrows, pigeons and ducks before graduating to full-blown goose.

ATTITUDE

Having the Right Attitude is thought by Adults to mean being V. Eager, perlite Etck. Certainly, behaving decently to fellow folk helps a lot in LIFE but in Koolspeak having lots of Attitude means, well, being Kool.

See also POSING.

CHAPTER TWO
BBBBBBBBBZÆ

Father in deep depression having got to final stage (he says) of CITYSCAPE *only to find I'd turned it off without saving game, thus blowing weeks of painstaking research. Mother making pointed remarks to effect he could spend time researching novel or else writing for the* Slob *instead of the worthy papers he contributes to now, and therefore make a few quid Etck. Father's furious response to this interference somewhat stilled by Only Mother's crool observation that he now seems to have let himself go to extent of weeing himself whilst in drunken stupor. Kept quiet about lager bottle mishap Etck. Feel badly about this, however – may confess when Feeling Stronger or Only Mother about to evict Only Father Etck.*

My attempts with purple dye to assuage Benjy's fears re bath mat resulted in large indigo blobs all over bathroom walls and rest of floor (cork tiles). Bath mat itself remains resolutely puce. Benjy now convinced alien mat has been sick in bathroom. Mother insists I spend paltry savings on paint to repair damage (bang goes new navel-revealing outfit for film course).

Tonight is first night of the course. Sick with Worry re lack of knowledge of subject, nothing to wear Etck Etck. Aggy is coming back from skule with me to calm savage breast, help decide on wardrobe Etck.

Got back to find Father and Benjy both still in tears, Benjy refusing to go near bathroom at all until mat removed and Martian vomit cleared up. Mother insists I cannot go out until bathroom shinier than rap star's skull Etck. After half an hour of scrubbing, Aggy (oh Noble frend in need!) offered to finish on her own so I could go to New Directions. *How will I ever repay her?*

Arrive, V. Flustered, at vast municipal building resembling oversize Job Centre (shortly to be sold to grasping Capitalist thugs thus depriving us of Welfare State Etck). Ask man at door where to go. His response V. Rude. Baffled, but see below for explanation of Strange Behaviour.

Wend way tragickly through network of peeling corridors, stairs, lifts, dead ends Etck and finally come upon dazzling logo: NEW DIRECTIONS START HERE. *Nearly turn back but realize I will be laughing stock among Aggy and family if I return empty-headed, so nervously enter, V. Late. All eyes swivel to regard* moi – *strange creature-from-other-werld whose outfit (Kool black sweat-shirt available from El Chubb Enterprises) is embroidered with honest but unappealing sweat-stains and purple foam. Realize face may be in similar condition and have time only to register gleaming wooden floor, gleaming glare of tutor and four of the swivelling eyes – the deep dark soulful gaze of Adam Stone and the shallow dark haughty stare of Ms Navel from the library. Arg.*

Squeeze myself in beside a comforting-looking older woman of about 40, who rustles strangely as I brush past, and a V. Interllekshual looking needle of a cove who is furiously scribbling in a vast note-book which looks as if it might suddenly snap shut and eat him, like Venus Flytrap.

The lecturer introduces himself (for the second time, he mentions, glancing pointedly at moi) as Phil Sleeve MA B.Phil. RSC.

He'll talk, he says with grim satisfaction, for most of this evening. Practical werk next week. Hopes there won't be any more latecomers (glares at moi).

Then, in V. Toady Tones, he simpers that it is his delight to have the privilege of welcoming Candice Carthage from the Los Angeles Film School . . . daughter of most famous Hollywood director and already such a distinguished student in her own right . . . has won prize with first film at numerous festivals, an extraordinary achievement for one so young . . . great honour her father thought this Humble Course suitable for her Etck Etck.

Candice (you guessed who she is) allows a roseate flush to suffuse her damask mug.

Candice . . . lowering her forest of lashes . . .

Lowering her forest of lashes to sweep her carefully
sculpted cheek and winking (I swear it) at Adam
Stone, she murmurs modestly that it is only one of
many courses she is sampling for her thesis, adding
graciously that she is certain it will be among the
most enthralling.

An awestruck hush.

Is this really the daughter of Mogul Mogul
Junior the Third? Hollywood Leg End? Maker of
Mission Interminable, Relatives of the Lost Clerk,
Raiders of the Lost Armband, Erratic Quark *and*
the soon to be released Anville?

Adam Stone strains forward, his eyes twin oceans
of desire. Tutor wriggles playfully and for next half-
hour addresses all his remarks to Candice's navel.

He will begin with a brief, he hopes (sickening
wink at Candice), survey of the reasons we are all
here, although he must apologize for going over
old ground in the case of some advanced students
(grovelling smirk at Candice), he is sure that even
the most brilliant of men – and women (more ooz-
ing in Candice's direction) – had to start at, for
want of a better werd, the beginning (nervous gig-
gle, clearing of throat, wagging of tail Etck). And
where better to start than a child's experience of
the Silver Screen? . . . blah . . . blah . . .

I am just sobbing self to sleep in back row when
I am roused by a name . . . what is the loathsome
lecturer saying?

'. . . perhaps best encapsulated in the glorious
but tragickly undervalued children's classic, the

*story of the 10-year-old girl on a remote,
windswept Highland Island . . .'*

*Am I hearing things? Is he intoning a passage
from the book I got out of the library? Surely not?
But, yes!*

*My moment of redemption is near. Mr Sleeve may
not impress me, but it is my duty to impress him –
and, by so doing, win Adam Stone's admiration from
the clutches of Candice Carthage. Hyperventilating, I
gasp in reedy tones: 'Yes, and isn't it wonderful when
the salt of the popcorn bursts like a sunrise in her
mouth and the cinema darkens and . . .'*

'Goodness!' exclaims Mr Sleeve.

*I am aware of three pairs of eyes sweeping in my
direction; the dark waves of Stone, the penetrating
Carthage beam, the rheumy gaze of Sleeve.*

They are impressed.

*'You have read the book?' Sleeve glances at his
register.*

*'Scarlett, I see – obviously from a family of
cinema lovers. Of a sort, at any rate.'*

*To a flurry of sniggers, but without missing a
beat, Sleeve drones to a conclusion.*

My misery at being named after the heroine of
Gone with the Wind *has never scaled a more
exquisite moment of glume. My only mission at
this point is to get out of there in manner that
makes Sonic the Hedgehog look like Droopy Etck.
But although the voice of Granny Chubb, never far
away from my thoughts, whispers 'more haste, less
speed', it is too late. Cannonball Chubb has collided*

with her neighbour, the stout, motherly figure festooned with carrier bags, which turn out to carry cameras, lenses, zooms, projectors and every other cinematographic device known to moviedom, now skidding hazardously across suicidally polished wooden floor. Speculate on legging it, but blurt apologies and stoop to scoop up what I know to be the unsaveable remains of priceless camera.

There is a blinding flash of light. Darkness descends.

Dear Reader, has yr Hopeless Heroine fainted in despair, to be revived by the soft breath of Adam Stone upon her brow, and other vital bits? No such luck. She has tripped over a lighting cable and fused the building. By the time Mr Sleeve had enjoyed calming everybody down (especially Candice) and performed man-of-the-people routine on grumbling janitor carrying torch, Mrs Stout had retrieved most of her hardware (all miraculously undamaged, being made of pre-Planned Obsolescence materials) and exited cheerfully announcing that she had come to wrong class and was looking for place to photograph nude male models. (At this point another blinding flash, this time inside my apology for a brain, as I realize a double-entendre *in the course title. The man at the door as I came in must have thought I was asking the way to* Nude Erections . . .*)*

Exit of Mrs Stout and WW2-style blackout drama united the class in cheerful camaraderie while we all jotted down what we were supposed

*to bring in next week (for form's sake, as I knew I
would not be coming back, I borrowed Mr Needle's
biro and wrote it on the back of my hand, where it
mingled with the purple dye rather attractively).*

*I felt I could now slither out, never to return,
when I felt a hand on my shoulder. I turned to gaze
into the eyes (glowing orbs Etck) of Adam Stone.*

'Is this yours?'

'No! . . . um, yes.'

*How could I deny that the plastic bottle, whose
purple trail led across the otherwise gleaming floor,
up my stone-washed denim legs and into my
pocket, was in fact my bottle of dye? 'Oh, silly me.
It's my baby brother.'*

'Looks like Indigo Dream *to me.' And he
flashed a smile of such radiance that my heart flew
to entwine with his for eternity and we got married
that evening. Whoops.*

*In fact, he said, 'Cheerio then, see you next
week. Let's hope Sleeve doesn't roll up for the
practical.' He winked. I think. And disappeared
into the dusk, a vision of long-limbed grace with
undulating Beumb to match Etck.*

*I floated home on his wink and practised rolling
up T-shirt to reveal navel, but on contemplating
grey gritty bits embedded therein decided to pursue
own course to Erotic Charisma rather than borrow
methods of Lesser Mortals Etck. Found sparkling
bathroom, sleeping and placated Benjy, adoring
Rover and cheese sandwich with crusts cut off left
out by Only Mother. Little thingz mean a lot.*

I'm writing this V.V.V. Late at night, trying to make sense of my tangled emotions. 'See you next week, see you next week.' And that witty little throwaway thing about Sleeve, who he obviously didn't like. Maybe then he wasn't gazing adoringly at Candice Carthage??? But was that really a wink or did he have a fly in his eye?

Maybe I should go next week?

If so, must think of some witty pun about Sleeve to impress Adam. Drift into jumbled dreamland musing along these lines . . . 'For such a short Sleeve he certainly goes on too long . . . makes you want to give him a cuff . . . glad you're in a sleeveless vest, wish I cld say the same for the course . . .' Etck.

Arg.

BALLET

In my Darling Mother's childhood there were supposed to be two types of Gurl – the ones who liked Ballet and the ones who liked horses.

This seems still true today and there are plenty of Teenage Worriers whose main LIFE Dream is still to twirl about pointily in tulle, and if you don't know what tulle is then you probably like horses.

My own experience of Ballet was miserable, however: my V. Rich and V. Stingy Grandma Gosling forked out for me to have Ballet lessons when I was 7. My Father took a video of the Ballet class

I stick out like sore thumb of ogre on hand of elfin

NO KENNEL
10 puppies
to support

Christmas show the year I was 9, and it definitely proves that a hippo really can be crossed with a giraffe, whatever David Attenborough might say.

Despite the Ballet Mistress's determined attempts to plonk me right at the back and give me the absolute minimum to do, I stick out like sore thumb of ogre on hand of elfin. My stifled sobs can be heard on the sound track. Two years of misery ended when this film was shown to Grandma Gosling, who immediately withdrew the funds. The relief was enormous, but I have a small pair of pink satin ballet shoes wrapped in tissue paper under the debris of my clothes cupboard and one day – who knows? – some fawn-like descendant of my Union with Adam may step into them and dance on air . . .

See also DANCING.

BEGGAR

I often think when I see Beggars sitting in doorways looking V. Pathetick and holding even more Pathetick dogs on bits of string

a) There but for Fate go *moi* and
b) People in the Govt shld try it for a week and see what they think.

There is big campaign in the Media to convince you Beggars all have Rolls-Royces parked round the corner, houses with gravel drives in Essex Etck, but personally I do not believe this, and anyway the Enterprise Culchur which helped create so many Beggars is only based on selling people just about anything for as much dosh as you can, so why not sell people the idea that you're a starving homeless wretch?

When I am PM I will bring in a law that says everyone, wherever you come from, has to do a week's begging, like my Adored Father sez National Service used to be years ago.

Then

a) Begging wld not seem so threatening to fine upstanding citizens worried about Crime Wave, Moral Collapse Etck and

b) Everyone wld get a chance to see how other half lives, which might do some thingz to them they wld remember for LIFE.

BOTTOMS

Let us have a last look (sigh) at men's Bottoms, before they all have to start wearing dresses. You may doubt this, but it cld become V. Imp for Future of Yumanity, as lowered sperm count brought on, among other things, by the wearing of tight jeans threatens species Etck, although as far as I know the movement for men to wear frocks is still only limited to sections of the Gay Community. I think it cld catch on quite fast if Armani or someone went with it. I wouldn't mind seeing Adam in a scarlet chiffon sheath (writhe, phew) and since everyone seems to agree the future is female (I read some-where that 80% of the jobs created in the next 10

Boyz in Frocks Pt 2
Designs by Armani-Westwood-Chubb

years will go to Gurlz, who will then make up 44% of all professionals) I guess it's time for Boyz to be more like Gurlz rather than striving for us Gurlz to be more like them and make more bombs Etck.

New El Chubb slogan: 'BEUMBS NOT BOMBS!'

BROTHERS

I have mixed feelings about brothers. I have one big brother, Ashley, who is Perfect In Every Way, and a little one who is frightened of floors. Between an Angel and a Luny, what chance does a normal average Teenage Worrier have?

NB: Teenage Worriers with sisters have same probs, joyz Etck as far as I can see, except they borrow yr clothes more if you are a gurl. Er, on the whole.

Sibling rivalry starts young . . .

Picture
of
innocence
↓

Benjy thinking floor has turned into Loch Ness

BULLIES

Teenage Worriers and skulekids often think that
Bullies are only people who kick yr ball over the
fence (poss plural in the case of Male Teenage
Worrier, ha), tear yr bukes, turn skule into
Blackboard Jungle Etck. But there are Bullies
everywhere in LIFE because it is about making
yrself feel strong by hurting someone you think is
weaker, and meant to be a sign that you are hurt
yrself but don't want anyone to know. In my skule
they say 'don't bully the bully', ie, to whit: if you
victimize the Bully to get them to stop they just get

Victim   Bully

N.B. Appearance can be misleading

worse because it confirms their inner sense of how terrible they are anyway. I am often V. Sympathetick to this explanation. I am often also tempted to find an ex-member of the SAS thrown on scrap heap by Govt Cuts Etck, and get him to brush up on his undercover interrogation methods on some of the Bullies I know. This is a Base Emotion To Be Resisted, but is also something that happens. NB: it is *V.V. Important*, if you ARE bullied, to report it to your mum, dad, teacher Etck. Keep on about it until they do something, which should be soon.

BUSKERS

Who brighten up the streets and tubes in Inner Cities with their cheery renditions of V. Old pop songs Etck, and are consequently moved on and abused by officious folk who would presumably rather they just lived in cardboard boxes drinking meths or maybe entertaining their fellow inmates as members of the prison population, which at the rate thingz are going will soon be just about all of us. (Thinks: this is obviously the Master Plan. The Govt intends to put everybody in prison except themselves and their mates, treat alll werk as donated free to help prisoners learn to be decent citizens, thus increasing their earnings by 80 zillion%.)

When you are 18 you are officially allowed to busk (apart from getting moved on Etck, as above). I think it is worth all Teenage Worriers considering Busking as a career to help pay fees through Art School, University, Drama College Etck, which the Govt used to pay for in the Golden Olden Daze when our parents were but striplings Etck. In London's seething Covent Garden, frinstance, there's a bloke who jumps over matchboxes. This can't be *that* hard to learn, surely?

Busker Tips <u>NB. only if you're 18+</u>

1. Get a <u>**SKILL**</u> - cld be just spraying self gold and pretending to be Statue of Liberty ← (not OK re-allergies as convulsive sneezing diminishes stately effect).

2. Get a <u>**PITCH**</u>. Check bye-laws to avoid fines.

3. <u>BULLY the **AUDIENCE**</u> (nicely)

   e.g. "After the count of TEN I want to hear how LOUD you can cheer 1, 2, 3...10 (puny shout) - a beautiful talented bunch like you can do MUCH better". Soon audience will cheer v. loud which attracts more people. <u>THEN</u> you remind them this is your <u>LIVING</u> - "I could," you fib, "be playing West End Theatres, but I CHOOSE the streets, to have RAPPORT with my audience (or audient....) but I need JUST enough to keep me and my pet alive."

4. Get a <u>PET</u>. Cute but **skinny** (worm, stick insect). Not really. Pets need RESPECK. See ANIMALS.

5. Get the <u>DOSH</u> "So I don't want

anything from you, except what you
can afford. Put your hand in
your pocket After the Show
and give me what you think I'm
WORTH. NO MORE. Take your
money out of your pocket, FOLD
it" (Laughter) "No, honest, ONE
pound is enough".

6. Do Your <u>ACT</u>. Make it look
really HARD. Like the bloke who
gets off a straight jacket in 2 mins
when he could do it in 30 secs.

7. Pass round <u>HAT</u>. If you have
done act V. Badly you will get
old socks, bus tickets Etck. If
well, the World could be yr.
oyster.

L.Chubb's Audience. (But just
WAIT till I'm 18).

CHAPTER THREE
CCCCCCEEEEEZE

*11 phone calls later – 7 to Aggy, 4 to Hazel – a few
consultations with packs of cards, lucky rabbit's
foot, God Etck later . . . I have decided to be
independent minded, throw caution to the winds,
toss my bonnet over the windmill and attend next
week's film lesson. What have I got to lose? Only
my pride (er, self-esteem, sense of worth, notion of
Meaning in Void Etck. Gulp).*

*Must admit other factor was Hazel's V.V.V.V. Kind
offer to lend me her video camera to help with my
project on Urban Dekay. All I have to do is pay for
half an hour's worth of tape. She is going to let me
have it for two weeks!! Sometimes, I reflect sadly, it
is V. Nice to have the odd frend with dosh . . .*

*Spend whole of Saturday combing flea markets
for clothes and combing fleas out of Rover in
attempt to raise self-respect. Wish I could follow my
own excellent advice to stick to something V. Simple,
but desire to cover up strange twigs and branches
that sprout randomly as apologies for limbs from
scrawny trunk of Yrs Truely is overwhelming me.*

*Luckily on third trip to market am made to see
sense by loyal Aggy (if only she had equal sense*

about her own dear form and would throw away those lime-green culottes) and finally choose V. Understated T-shirt in Ebony with just the merest hint of Jet and some slinky trousers the colour of fog, with a faint luminous sheen. V. Pleased, despite guilt-pangs re spending hard-saved dosh on self, instead of GCSEs (Granny Chubb's Specs Endeavour).

Home with long-suffering Aggy to try various styles for wig. After three hours of coiling and plait-ing we decide dreadlocks do not suit blotchy Chubb complexion so Aggy gets out iron and irons each corkscrew straight. As she pulls last strand of wig into agonizing scorching tautness, I am aware of large drops of water plopping onto ironing board.

Has my Only Mother invested in a steam iron? Has Only Father been fixing plumbing again? No, the drops of water are the tears of dear Aggy, who is remembering how her mother used to iron her frizzy mop when she was 10, in the halcyon days before she ran off with the postman.

Poor Aggy, lumbered with tearful, though caring, father and so many siblings I can never remember all their names . . . Do I care only for myself? Am I the person who vowed to devote LIFE to Nunnery, Art Etck and forsake Sins of Flesh? Spend next three minutes comforting Aggy and offer to make her cheese sandwich. Sadly, no cheese or bread in house but she tearfully accepts half a digestive biscuit before going home to cook for the small village that resides in her father's two-bedroom flat.

Resolve to divert some of earnings as film director

into improving Aggy's lot before plunging through my old portfolio of photographs in order to find a selection worthy of taking to the film course. Need Angle that might werk up into Project. Sleeve has requested that we bring a storyboard of ideas along and he will choose the best three for us all to collaborate on. I decide that Urban Deprivation is burning issue and that pics of Granny Chubb eating tin of cat food (or possibly cat, though Rover may need fee in excess of Tom Cruiser earnings to pose for same), tramp with dog on string and V. Harrowing pic of Aggy taking 4 little siblings to skule on misty morning will form basis of Grate Werk.

Jot down few ideas re gap between Rich and poor ever-widening (worst in Western World, according to posh newspaper written by caring interllekshuals who shake heads over areas like mine from windows of Volvo estates) and fall into bed convinced of future fame, fortune Etck.

CAFFEINE

It always surprises me how parents let their little diddums kiddies eat all kinds of junk they wouldn't dream of feeding to their pets, viz: 'Don't you dare give Fido a chocolate biscuit, you know it'll make his coat dull, his nose dry, he'll get hyperactive and stay out all night at Raves Etc.'

But while Fido, Puss and the goldfish are fed with stringent rigour, little Darren and Karen are stuffed with Caffeine, fizz and sugar, starch and bubbles. They zoom into acned adolescence at a serious dietary disadvantage in the humble opinion of El Chubb, Dietary Adviser to Divorced Members of Royal Family Etck.

On *le autre main* you get loads of kids who have eaten nought but bread you need a fork-lift truck to carry, lentils, rice Etck until they turn into yuman beanbags (even at *parties*, where the 'sweeties' are sultanas, grue, yeech, puke Etck), who are frequently weedier, spottier, paler and infinitely more glumey than their mates.

'It's all a question of balance,' as my dear old Primary Skule Teacher, Miss Scales (how I miss her), used to say.

Caffeine is also unique in ye Drug Culchur (along with tannin, which is what's also in tea, and coats yr insides with something like boot polish if Granny Chubb's teapot is anything to go by) for being socially acceptable, even at church fêtes. Suppose Conservative Ladies called their fund-raising gatherings 'Caffeine Mornings'? What wld happen to attendance?

'A nice fix of tannin, Vicar?'

Wheel on the soft drugs trolley and LIVE!

See DIETS for El Chubb's perfectly balanced nutrition guide for today's Yoof.

CAMPAIGN

'Campaign' has several meanings – there are Campaigns in wars, when muddy, cursing V. Unhappy Boyz with guns spend months, or maybe years, trying to win back one molehill with a V. Baffled looking mole standing on it off the other side and call it a Glorious Victory, Turning Point in History Etck. There are also Election Campaigns, which are also about trying to win said molehill off the other side, but without guns (usually). But the kind of Campaigning most interesting for Teenage Worriers is where you choose something you are V. Passionate About (preferably The Environment, The Beumb, The Planet, Animal Rights Etck rather than Brad Pittbull) and try to Get Something Done About It.

Why do this? I hear you cry, in breathless anticipation . . . because

a) It may be good for the Yuman Race, future generations Etck

b) It is a way of DOING rather than WORRYING.

CAREER

As you know, dearest reader, I am V. Lucky in already having chosen my career as werld famous film director, but what to do after skule is V. Big Worry for many.

A Career used to mean doing the same job for LIFE, with a bit of luck getting better paid at it until they give you a gold-plated Zimmer frame. Now it means just staying on yr feet however many times they pull the rug out from under you. In which respeck, it seems to me the word Career has now come closer to its other meaning, as in 'careering toward the precipice' Etck.

El Chubb's advice for the 21st century is: make the most of Yoof while you have it, learning anything that might turn out to be useful later, and staying at skule as long as poss. Since there is no such thing as olde-fashioned job security, you will need to re-invent yourself every few years anyway, so it is a V. Good Idea to learn one thing: HOW TO THINK.

Werld Leaders Etck find this task V. Difficult.

It is V. Imp to remember the famous saying of Eric Cantona – sorry, René Descartes: 'I think, therefore I am,' or '*cogito ergo sum*' in Latin. It is closely related to the famous philosopher El Chubb's theory '*agito ergo sum*' or 'I Worry, therefore I am'. Descartes thought this up about 350 years ago, and apart from the fact that it might cause a few politicians and pop groups a few moments of doubt that they actually exist, it probably doesn't seem that much of a big deal to the rest of us these days.

Anyway, back to Careers. Careers Advisers at skule will be V. Helpful in telling you what you need to study to go in your desired direction Etck but it cld be worth finding out what the job prospects are at the end and nothing beats personal experience. So, if you want to be a Marine Biologist, try and MEET some of them and find out what the job is really like, and I bet they don't all play the harmonica and teach whales basketball Etck either.

See also JOBS, WORK.

CAR-WASHING

This is a job often done by Yoof in search of a few pennies for the next handful of dried grape-pips for dinner Etck. People sometimes prefer younger Car-washers than Teenage Worriers, unfairly suspecting the latter of using it as a cover to steal the radio Etck, but then regret this decision when two dripping Infants come to the door for their money while car looks as if it has been rallying in Outer Mongolia. Car-washing can be done at traffic lights, but this is not advisable, as people tend to drive off with you on the bonnet, threatening to start campaign in *Daily Wail* about you if you complain. Proper technique for Car-washing is: hose or splash car all over to shift grime, encourage it to dislodge with a soft brush, rinse off with clean water, then wipe dry with a clean chamois leather.

We can learn from the younger generation

You can intersperse into this activity

1) Hose down partner

2) Forget to close door whilst hurling bucket of water at car

3) Miss car and hit passing escaped maniac instead Etck.

CATS

My Adored Father walled Rover up once. He was
rewiring the house, a job that seemed to take about
10 years and through which we mostly sat in the
dark with no telly, and took turns to do impressions
from *EastEnders*, *Top of the Pops*, Etck. Adored
Father made a lot of unnecessarily large holes in
cavity wall upstairs, Rover got in for a quiet snooze
to escape from sound of Benjy thinking floor had
turned into bird's nest soup, Adored Mother railing
on about Medieval Living Conditions Etck; after
various flashes, bangs, curses Etck Adored Father
plastered up holes and suddenly we had the Cheshire
Cat disappearing to leave only his grin, except that
Rover disappeared to leave only her piteous whinge.

I mention this to draw yr attention to a famous
feature of Cats, viz Curiosity. Cat lovers like *moi* do
not like to contemplate the thought that Cats may do
these things out of Stupidity rather than Curiosity,

and I agree with the Egyptians, who made gods
and goddesses out of Cats and did statues of them
adopting V. Sensible flattering policy of making them
look much taller and slimmer than they really are,
a wise investment for a Good Deal in the After LIFE.

CELIBACY

Celibacy is Not Doing It. You wld not believe that
anybody of legal age except Persons of God are in
this position, or non-position, if you pay a lot of
attention to the tabloid newspapers – or, for that
matter, even the posh newspapers now, which are
just as desperate to mention SEX whenever possible
(unlike El Chubb, ahem).

Though the coverage of SEX in the papers, on
telly Etck now makes it seem as if the whole nation is
At It all day and all night, I don't believe it *moi*self.
This is not just El Chubb rationalization at work. I
just think people are beginning to find SEX much
more interesting in the papers or on the Internet, or
down the telephone than they do in Real LIFE.
Perhaps this is the Safe SEX we hear so much about.

If you are Celibate as a Statement about
Respeck, Waiting for Real Lurve Etck, then nobody
thinks the worse of you and it can be helpful to
ruminate on Spiritual rather than Carnal pleasures.
V. Useful while still at skule, as thinking about
SEX, Boyz Etck is wrecking my concentration.

CELLULITE

El Chubb never wants to hear this word again. But for those of you who missed the pix of that famous supermodel (tee hee Etck), it means fatty deposits around the thighs that make yr skin look dimply and blobby. No one except an obscure handful of medics had heard of that thing that rhymes with smellubite until V. Recently when advertisers saw their chance to make fortunes by telling us all how to get rid of it. Even the photographer who took the photos of the model didn't know what it was! His WIFE spotted it! This could be deemed an act of treachery to womankind, but I s'pose it was hard to resist the temptation to sell the photos for a fortune. El Chubb wld never be so corrupt with my tender moving photos of G. Chubb and Aggy Etck. At any rate, now we all DO know about it, even Teenage Worriers are Worrying about it! Grrrrr, rage, snarl.

CELLULITE FACTS:
All adult women and lots of Teenage Worriers have fat on their thighs. This is how it should be, and is part of Yuman adaptation to environment Etck.

Some look more dimply than others. So do some cheeks. So what? (I LIKE dimples.)

You can read every day in every daft magazine about creams, gels, leeches (not *really*, just checking you're concentrating), scrubs, rub-a-dub dubs Etck, all of which are V. Expensive and none of which work for more than about three seconds.

Work on what, anyway? Do you really want a giant eraser to rub yrself out?

CENTAUR

Attractive beast, half-man, half-horse. Could this be what we all want really?

Is this what we all want really?

CHESS

More interllekshual Teenage Lurvers might consider giving Chess a break. It is not only played by pointy-heads with hair like bursting mattress Etck, but also

by all of those who know that mental proximity is
as important as physical proximity and anyway the
one can lead to the other, or The Other, as my
Adored Father still unbelievably sez. After all, it has
lots of Romantick Stuff in it, knights, castles, mating
Etck. Unfortunately it also has pawns in it, but it
was invented a long time ago, before European
Court of Yuman Rights Etck, and one has to take it
with pinch of salt since in many ways Chess otherwise resembles the evolution of Teenage LIFE, viz, to
whit: cautious early moves backwards, forwards and
sideways Etck, deception about Real Intentions,
eventual cornering of Lurve Object and inescapable
conclusion of MATE. Sigh, swoon, Worry Etck . . .

CHRISTMAS

Alas and Woe for the passing of innocent childhood when all you wanted was a Fluorescent Pony
with Wings and a Machine Gun with Rotating
Bayonet Attachment. What you forget is that you
never got the first because it was soppy and you
never got the second because it was violent and all
you got was krap like edukashunal jigsaws made of
real wood where the pieces didn't fit. Not really –
my parents weren't quite this barmy. But I must
admit that, although Christmas isn't as exciting as
it was when you propped your eyelids open to wait
for the big bloke in the red suit (terrified you might

REALLY see him), I still have deeply cosy feelings at this time of year.

OK, I like trees, tinsel, glitter, chortling robins Etck and enjoy cherubic face of Benjy as he hangs up stocking. Fact that cherubic face dissolves in tears V. Soon on realizing no Machine Gun with Bayonet Attachment, Lifesize Virtual Reality Football Pitch or Real Working Moon-Rocket emerges from stocking next morning does not diminish El Chubb's feeling of hopefulness at this time of year. Could be that it's 'cos everyone stops doing something else and you are allowed to wear V. Silly hats, slippers Etck and play komputer games for 10 hours without being nagged . . . (I mean go to Church, ponder on Life's Mystery, Spiritooality Etck).

CLASS SYSTEM

The Class System is V. Imp to LIFE in Britain, and people get V. Worried about it for the V. Good reason that it seems designed to make sure only one type of person (rich people) get the breaks and everyone else has to stay out of the ditch as best they can.

Long ago, Barons, Dukes, Earls Etck plundered the land and put up big signs over vast swathes of Ye Countryside saying 'MINE'. Their descendants built a lot of V. Pretty skules in green rural idylls, flash parts of town Etck, for their own children to go to, so they cld share tips about Plundering, Exploiting,

Pillaging, Shouting Etck. They also evolved V. Secret Code for addressing each other (*orffff*, ie: Off; *Gawlff*, ie: Golf; *Hice*, ie; House Etck) so they cld keep the best bits to themselves without Ye Peasants knowing where they were off to.

In the Class System there used to be three groups – Upper Clarse, Middle Class and Werkin' Class. This is now changing because most of the hammering, bashing, digging, swearing Etck jobs are now being done by robots and large parts of the Werking Class aren't at werk, so the title seems a bit daft. Also, the Upper Clarses have spent all

Toffspeak for: 'He's gone into the house.'

Prolespeak for same

their money on horses, paintings, Olde Retainers Etck, and have been forced to sell a lot of their best stuff to Lean, Hungry, Snapping Middle Classes On Way Up, so we may be moving to a new Class System which is just Middle Class and Underclass like in America. These things are V. Complicated, and can make Yr Brain Hurt after a while.

CLUBS

Adored Mother and Father used to go to Klubs

about a million years ago when they were young and carefree (cld such a thing be possible, I ask *moi*-self?) and go on about how they heard Dire Straits in the days when they were all still skuleteachers or newsagents or something, standing as-close-as-I-am-to-you-now-and-Mark-had-a-strat-just-like-the-one-I-had-a-cardboard-replica-of Etck, yawn, cringe.

This seems to be exactly why they can't stand the Klubs Teenage Worriers go to today – it's all different now, you must all be raving mad, the places we went to were about music, not brain-scrambling noise, people behaved like Yuman Beans, cld have a quiet chat over a drink in a corner Etck. I know for a fact that Adored Father was banned from several Klubs in his locality as a Yoof, once for dancing so close to the stage he stuck his head through a loudspeaker, once for spitting at a bouncer in the mistaken impression that he was a famous punk star who would treat it as a cheery greeting.

But it's true that Klubs are different now, and though I'm too young to visit them (you've really got to be 18, or at least LOOK it, unlike pubs), the Klubbing werld has become as much a part of Yoof Culchur as pop bands, fanzines and clothes.

One of the V. Exciting things about Klubbing is that, like most really new developments in Pop, the inspiration for the best stuff came from the people who Do It, not a bunch of ex-hippies in white suits at a big record company. The danger now is that said record companies have realized how much money there is in Klubbing and are trying to take it all over and turn it into one massive Disco Disneywerld with everything interesting blanded out just the way they like it.

Parents like this better, of course, because they Worry that Klubland is full of Ecstasy-selling gangsters and can't wait for the day when the whole thing is organized like theme parks and there are franchises selling E-Burgers with ingredients

← Veg 'E' burger approved by Dept. of Health

approved by the Dept of Health, Virtual Reality DJs for the day when the Big Names are too expensive to bother to turn up in person any more, actors dressed as drug-dealers pretending to kill each other in the loos Etck. The balance between a risky werld created by Teenage Worriers so they both Have Fun and Worry in ways that aren't run by their parents or the Govt, and a werld in which you're no more likely to get killed or go mad than you wld be working the checkout in Sainsbury's is hard to get, but all the panicky stuff parents are told in the *Daily Wail* Etck certainly doesn't help.

Klubbing is mostly (I am told) about music and dancing and Having a Gd Time, and only a small bit about drugs, dume, glume Etck, the things that Teenage Worriers have to use their common sense about everywhere today, not just in the Toxic Rat.

To keep up with what's going on (because it keeps changing every 5 minutes – Drum 'n' Bass, which does sound like being in a washing machine, but with a lot of knives and forks rattling around inside as well, is currently bigger than House but *moi* prefers Funk and Soul) it's a good idea to read the Klubbing magz, espesh the letters columns, which tell you a lot about how people just like you are feeling about this confusing scene. They're all V. Determined to stop the Klub scene falling into the hands of the Theme-Parkers and Disco-Multiplexers, and I only hope they can keep it up until El Chubb looks flash enough to lie to the bouncers about her age – some hopes Etck.

See MUSIC.

COMPUTERS

No Guide to LIFE wld be complete without considering Komputers because they have taken over many aspecks of our Lives, viz, to whit: there are many Boyz I wld say definitely prefer relationships with their Komputers to relationships with Gurlz, maybe it will only be a matter of time before they look like Lara Croft and as a matter of fact I don't think Pammy has so far given us any proof that she isn't a Komputer anyway, playing a V. Long Boring Game called *Boom & Bust*. Come to think of it, perhaps they cld make Komputers that look like Adam, with all necessary working parts including V. Super-developed (wait for it) Eternal Devotion programme networked to El Chubb@paradise.phew.steam.co.uk.

CONTRACEPTION

sadly, my detailed drawings of Teenage Worriers attempting to use condoms Etck. have been censored. But make sure you use one plus spermicide + diaphragm if poss if you have SEX. See SEX.

CHAPTER FOUR
DDDDDDZÆ

Day 2 of film course.

Sick with Worry, saunter nonchalantly up steps, and casually lope past Adam Stone, who luckily cannot hear (I think) the herd of horses galloping beneath my breastbone. Am just about to drop my portfolio casually at his feet – and imagining his graceful bend to help me collect my work, giving him an opportunity to gasp with admiration at my heartfelt observations on Inner City deprivation – when am pounced on by Mr Needle, demonstrating priorities of A1 Nerdishness by demanding the return of his biro.

Have naturally mislaid same and am forced to give him my V. Nice pen (Only Father's actually, though he now claims he can't write without a komputer, and due to CITYSCAPE can't write with one, either), leaving me with nothing to take notes.

During this encounter I spy out of the corner of my eye that Candice is gliding up to Adam and engaging him in intense, meaningful conversation using twin-barrelled assault of mouth and naval simultaneously. Her top is also cut both high and low at the same time, I am sorry to report, and

*establishes that she has no need of a Wonderbra.
Nachurally, all three of her secure a place next to
Adam.*

*My misery is compounded by the following event.
Sleeve is looking through the portfolios.*

He pauses, clearly amazed. 'Whose is this?'

*'Mine,' I cry proudly, the horses once more
fretting their proud hooves in my gurlish breast.*

*'Fascinating,' he murmurs. 'Oh joy! He's going
to demonstrate the poetic, penetrating, profound,
pulverizing insights of the works of Yrs Truely to
the class!*

He shows them page after page.

Page after page.

It's Benjy's school work.

The life sickle of a tatpole.

Mi day at the zoooo.

Hou a plarnt wercks.

And so on.

And on.

*I remember my Mother buying those identical
portfolios at her art class summer sale. But how
could I have picked up Benjy's?*

*'Were we thinking of cinéma naïf? A new form?'
asks the sadistic Sleeve. 'Or is your project purely
domestic?'*

I run from the room in confusion.

Even the noble Aggy is unable to comfort me.

*Cry all night and next day I see Adam Stone at
my usual bus stop! He is talking to Candice
Carthage. Misery, glume, sackcloth, ashes. Hide*

behind hedge and miss bus. Late for skule. Woe.
Dume. Must throw self into werk . . .

DAMSEL

Don't climb!
It's a wig

Damsels in Distress are s'posed to be V. Weedy
types holed up in towers waiting to let their hair
down to V. Nimble Laid-Back Princes who always
just happen to be walking in woods miles from
anywhere and hear the tragic cry of ye Damsel in
Distress, viz: 'Woe is me' Etck.

Alternatively Ye Damsels are sitting in castles
weaving webs of pure gold out of wire wool,
emptying oceans with sieves Etck until RESCUE.
In ye Olden Daze it might have been sensible for
gurlz to sit around waiting for someone to get
them out of a hole, but there should be no need to
be a Damsel in the 21st century, and there aren't
so many chances to be a Damsel in Distress these
days anyway, unless you just stand around at the
roadside in a short skirt in hysterics because you
don't know which end of yr car the engine's in.
My Adored Father always keeps an eye open for
this type of Damsel as he goes about his benighted
way, but he doesn't have much luck, and El Chubb
suspects this might be 'cos they're a dying breed.

However, there are other kinds of Damsels in
Distress in the 21st century: they just aren't the kind

GREAT THOUGHTS of EL Chubb No. 128: Wonder if 'Damsel' came from 'Damn cell' as Rapunzel, sleeping Beauty Etck. cursed their lonely towers, bowers, Etck....

that gets noticed by my Adored Father – or any other adored (or unadored) father (or mothers, come to that). Much as I wld like to say, if in distress, take evasive action (like bopping wicked step-parents on hooter and leaving home for wide welcoming werld) things have not changed so much for Teenage Worriers as we would like to think. Many of us are still holed up with V. Overprotective parents or else are Not Cared About At All (which, believe me, is much worse). However, it *is* V. Imp not to expect some gorgeous BOY to appear and solve your probs (except in the case of *moi* and Adam) as if you have lots of probs, you are unlikely to be in the mood for

Lurve anyway and the last thing that a 21st century boy wants to do is support a family when he isn't ready to, especially his own.

DANCE

Gone are the daze, sighs my Hopeless romantick Only Mother, when swave blokes in DJs swirled elegant partners disguised as lampshades round glistening parquet to string quartets Etck. They did things like waltzes, fox-trots (always makes me think of quadruped with the runs), polkas, gavottes Etck and filled their dance cards like in those old Jane Austen films (I mean, bukes, ahem). In fact, this kind of Dancing went out of fashion when Granny Chubb was a gurl and I don't believe my Only Mother ever did it, although she seems to think she might have, if she'd stayed in High Society instead of dropping out with my dear Only Father.

The only Old Dancing I Lurve and feel V. Jealous of is Jive and I wish I could learn all that jumping over heads and jitterbugging like in old Elvis movies. Other OK trad types are Scottish, Country and Tap as performed by V. Grate and Trooooly Kool Stars like Fred Astaire, Ginger Rogers Etck.

What bugs *moi* a bit is it is V. Hard to know exactly what to do when Dancing. I like to, er, go with the beat Etck but unfortunately the beat

L. Chubb's Dance
(to tune of *Hokey Cokey*)
NB: Stage 4 is not possible for average human,
but it's fun to try.
After stage 8, start again with right elbow,
knees, hands, feet Etck.

– and that's what it's all ABOUT

doesn't stay with *moi*. It could be that I'm just one of those two-left-foot types who would have plonked about in any period of Dance History, but I feel the need of some help with this to stop lurking V. Embarrassed in dark corners while everyone else lets it all hang out Etck. Slinky swinging of hips is best I have achieved so far.

See BALLET, CLUBS and MUSIC.

DAY-DREAMING

A day without Dreams is like a day without sunshine, sez *moi*. Can you imagine being unable to IMAGINE?

If you are a genuine Teenage Worrier, you will waste quite a lot of Day-dream time with Worrying . . . ie: gazing nervously at yr spots and wondering will they ever go, will anyone like you with them or without them Etck. But Day-dreaming ends all this. In it, you fantasize about doing all yr favourite things with all yr favourite people.

Ie: One of my Day-dreamz wld be lying in a bath of warm liquid fudge with Adam and licking . . . [CENSORED] . . . after which I wld win Pulitzer Prize for fudge-wallowing and have werld at my feet. That sort of thing. Quite modest.

But Day-dreaming can be quite low-key and free-associating. You can just gaze emptily into

Just some of my favourite daydreams.
Others that I'd like – to be a BOY (espesh in changing
rooms, heh heh) or a famous detective

The QUALITY ....

PM INTRODUCES NEW LAWS TO FAVOUR YOUTH

Prime Minister Letty Chubb announced today that her government would declare
• ZERO TOLERANCE for poverty.
• FREE homes and travel passes for all.
• Communal bikes and roller blades available at all tube and bus stations.
Turn to page three to see L.Chubb's 20 point plan in full

L. Chubb drifts whimsically above glades of fancy

space and let your thoughts roam free. As long as you allow your thoughts to drift whimsically among the glades of fancy and invention (never plunging into Worry-land) you will wake from your Day-dream truely refreshed.

Lots of experiments have been done about the dangers of depriving people of Dreaming Sleep, but El Chubb's belief is that it is equally important to provide Dreaming Daze and that anyone bereft of opportunities for same will sink into glume. However, you have to use this information carefully. Parents, teachers Etck can become V. Grumpy when you say you are lying on the sofa in a week-old pair of socks watching *Neighbours* because it helps reconnect you with Yr Vital Subconscious Etck.

DEPRESSION

Glume, melancholy, long periods spent sobbing into pillow – all these are Part and Parcel of a Teenage Worrier's LIFE. But real lasting Depression, like when you know you should be pleased that the sun is shining but you can't remember why, because you can't feel pleasure, is serious. No one should have to put up with feeling like that and it is important to get help. People talk V. Disparagingly about therapy or about 'Happy pills', but both these things save lives and are essential tools for recovery.

Many many people have tried one or the other to get them out of a hole and then found that they never need them again. So don't Worry that if you need treatment for Depression it is going to be a LIFElong thing. But do see your doc, fast.

See also PSYCHIATRISTS.

DIETS

EL CHUBB'S DIET TIPS:

1. Eat what you like.
2. Eat when you're hungry.
3. Never read any diet tips except these.

IF everybody had always followed this excellent advice, sez Dr Chubb, then we wouldn't have tens of thousands of miserable Teenage Worriers suffering from Eating Disorders and wishing they looked like Kate Moss.

BUT

(this is my big 'but', not to be confused with the dieter's big butt), it obviously ain't quite that simple.

Why? Because we've all been bullied about food over the years:

'You can have your pudding after you've finished

all your greens' . . . 'Think about the Starving
Children in Poor Countries' . . . 'Oooooh! MORE
choccy cake! You *naughty* thing' . . .

Then, after a dozen or so years of being made to
eat everything on our plates whether we liked it or
not, we're told to watch our weight. ARG.

No wonder we're confused.

But if over a third of Teenage Gurlz in Britain
(some say as many as 42% – *which is nearly HALF
of us!!!!!!*) are Worried about their weight to the
extent of going on DIETS – then we have a *Big*
problem.

Fact is, we need food, we need good food, we
need plenty of it. It is making us strong, healthy
and clever.

You need loads of vitamins, protein and minerals
and you can get them by eating loads of healthy
food.

COUNTING CALORIES

A calorie is a unit of heat. Which means energy.
Some food has more, some less. Counting
calories does not help you find out whether the
food has other good stuff in it, like minerals
and vitamins. It is also so V. Boring. Can you
imagine counting leaves on a hedge? But
magazines are badgering our mothers to do this
on every news stand. And Teenage magz and
TV programmes do the same by presenting us
with pics of UNREAL gurlz.

Eat some of these
each day to be
- HEALTHY -

Some DAIRY-ish bits.
(cheese, yoghurt, milk)
~~TWICE~~ a day.

MEATISH or SEED-ish bits.
(nuts, fishy-stuff, a nice
eggy, chicky or red meat).
2 or 3 times a day. Could be
peanut butter, f'rinstance.

VEGGIES
Kool cucumber, beans!
Brocolli (v.v. good for you).
Carrots! Etck. 2 or 3 times.

BREAD-ish stuff.
Pasta! Rice! Buns!
Cereal! LOADS.

L. Chubb's healthy eating guide

AND FRUIT!

"Oh, handsome doctor,"
All the gurlies say:
"We never eat an APPLE
'cos it keeps the doctor away"

TWO fruits a day.
And BEANS!
DRINK plenty of water.

JOIN EL.Chubb's
CAMPAIGN against
Mineral Water.

CAMPAIGN for
CLEAN TAP water for all!

NEVER forget to
grate FUDGE on your
SALAD

Perfectly Simple . . .

Campaign for Real Gurlz in all their blobby, stringy, knobbly, floppy, fluffy, gritty, daffy, dottiness! Real Gurlz are Brill!

I'm burbling on about this at some length 'cos I now realize how many gurlz are obsessed with their weight and it is ruining their lives. In fact my own prob is I always wanted to be fatter (so I don't go straight up and down and look like a fireman's pole) but I am beginning to realize that just as we all have different colours, noses, talents, dreamz, Etck, so we are all different weights and your natural body weight is what you will get if you just eat and exercise sensibly and enjoy it.

If you are seriously obese and/or very tired, it could be a medical condition like an underactive thyroid, so it is worth asking the doc to check this and anything else out. Don't be fobbed off. Get a blood test (especially if you are also tired). But if you are just plumper than average, who really cares? What is average anyway? (Size 16, so there: that means half the women in Britain are size 16, a quarter are over and a quarter are under.)

Dieting doesn't work. It makes you cold (lack of energy), depressed (lack of fun), it makes you thick (mentally, not physically – it deprives the brain of nutrients). It makes money for ruthless Diet-mongers and advertisers – and it makes for depression in Teenage Worriers.

See also EATING DISORDERS and EXERCISE.

DISABILITIES

Most Teenage Worriers are convinced that they
are riddled with abnormalities of one kind or
another – noses, willies, bazooms Etck too big,
not big enough. This kind of Worrying can feel
as though it is blighting yr LIFE. But the kind of
disabilities that actually render you incapable of
doing most of the things in this buke are the
serious ones, so stop whingeing for once (wish I
could) if you have sight, hearing and a working
pair of arms and legs.

Sometimes it might be qu. good for the soul to
pause to ponder on the fortunes of those who don't
have all the werking parts, like Sylvie, the gurl at
my Primary Skule who had Cerebral Palsy and was
sent on to a 'Special Skule' when she was 11 'cos
Sluggs Comprehensive wouldn't take her. Sylvie
could walk a bit (with crutches) and talked using a
machine that sounded a bit like a Dalek. But she
was V.V.V.V.V. Clever and prob got V. Bored in her
Special Skule. I never kept in touch with her. I
think I'll ring her up now (lash guilt moan).

There *has* been progress recently for better
access Etck and if you have disabilities you can
now do Wheelchair Olympics and suchlike, but
the most important thing is to feel a Proper Person
and not someone who is just identified as blind
(or 'visually impaired' or 'differently abled' or
whatever the fashionable phrase is).

DOGS

If Rover sees me recommending Dogs I'm afraid she'll have a panic attack and leave home. My secret desire to have a Dog is therefore best-kept secret in town so I cannot reveal it even to you, tender Reader. However, many Teenage Worriers unburdened by (I mean, not privileged to own) cats, yearn for a pooch to call their own and some even have mogs that co-exist happily with dogs. I guess there are houses where parents are quite happy about the many exotic mixes of furs and smells that arise from a cosy collaboration between the feline and the canine, but sadly the House of Chubb is not one.

Dogs come in three basic types:

Bunny
rabbit
slippers

LASSIE (dog-of-your-dreams).

usually owned by small, yapping, lady

YAP!
YAP!
yip yip
yip yip
yip yip
yip yip
yippety
YAP!

FROU FROU

FANG

DRAMA

All Teenage Worriers act and most, let's be heart-breakingly honest, are Drama Queens. Gurlz and Boyz pose before mirrors for hours in vain attempt to simulate Tom Cruiser, Brad Pittbull, Gwyneth Paltry Etck, usually by adopting Visage like person torn between conflicting sensations of Erotic Trance and Seasickness, in hope of getting on fast track to flame and gory.

El Chubb hates to disillusion any Stagestruck Worrier with boring, Adult-type statistics, but, like yr Elders and Worsers are bound to tell you at some point, 92% of actors are out of werk at any one time. That means 8% of actors are marching around shouting famous lines from Spokeshave, being filmed thrashing around in sack with Sharon Grone, Tom Spews Etck, fighting animatronic dinosaurs, blowing things up Etck, and the rest are languishing on dole.

Since even the 8% who are werking all the time are V.V. Insecure and spend all their time Worrying if enough people have noticed them, this means they never stop and they go on taking werk that the other 92% wld really like – frinstance a nice little voice-over on an advertisement for mashed potato that anyone cld do, but it always goes to a Famous Voice. The message is: 'Eat mashed potato and get as big a house/car/willy/bank balance/fan club as Sean Beanpole. It worked for him, why not you?'

Forgive me, gentle Reader, for introducing a note of cynicism here. I, too, have my Dreamz, but when you look like a hairpin and sound like a sparrow you have to be realistic, hence I will be werld-famous director instead (ahem), though I may consider becoming a Character Actor in middle age, ie: about 25.

Those of you keen to tread boards, smell grease-paint Etck shld definitely have a go while you are still at skule. Most skules (even Sluggs) have Drama groups and end of year productions and it will give you some idea of whether your germ of talent can be nurtured. Viz: if you are too shy to stand up in front of Ms Drizel the Drama Teacher and spout the Bard, you will not fare well at the National Theatre.

DRUGS

Apart from caffeine (see CAFFEINE) and tannin, most drugs are illegal. Being scared of

a) The Law and
b) The effects

is good enough reason to steer clear in humble opinion of El Chubb. But everyone does it, they say. Not so. Even at Druggs – I mean Sluggs – Comprehensive, where they are available to Year 7s like sweeties and men in baseball caps and long mackintoshes hang around outside the playground or send in innocent kids to sell them, even THERE in the cesspit of Urban Dekay Etck *most* of my frenz aren't taking anything. Lots of others are, of course. But increasingly you get respeck for saying 'No' as the Drug Culchur is getting less Kool as more people see their elder cousins, siblings Etck cracking up (literally) from having over-indulged.

Not so much is known about newer drugs, but psychotic behaviour, hallucinations, possible brain damage, depression and kidney damage are real possibilities. As is a terminal visit from the Grim Reaper.

My Aged Father is deeply hypocritical about this – 'Don't do as I do, do as I say' Etck. But I think too much dope in his student days is prob the reason he is now reduced to staring vacantly at *CITYSCAPE* for aeons. Must check this with doc. Also V. Worried whether I had too much Calpol, antibiotics Etck as Baby and am now prey to Killer Viruses Etck. Worry, Worry.

LEGAL DRUGS!
Favoured abuse-systems of adult werld
(though fags giving way to gum).

CHAPTER FIVE
EEEEEEZZE AND
FFFFFFZE

Have left house excruciatingly early for four whole days in order to avoid dread bus stop and possible nightmarish vision of Adam Stone entwined with Candice Carthage. Know it's crazy when have only spoken two words to him, but confidence at low ebb Etck.

However, this a.m. was V. Late – as usual no kind parent offering lift because

a) Apology for car not working (apology for Father has removed gearbox and left it with No Problem Mate *garage, who now don't return his phonecalls about it).*

b) Even if it was working Only Father wld deliver lecture about how he walked 6 miles to skule and all he ate was a piece of toast and dripping which had to last him a week.

To cut a short story long, decide to take courage in both flippers and get usual bus. Probably wouldn't see Adam anyway, who cares if I do, just another

*bloke Etck Etck. Leap full tilt onto bus, hooking
strap of bag round bus conductor's upraised
warning arm, hurl Self into last remaining seat,
dragging bus conductor unwillingly into V.
Embarrassing head In Lap pose. In said circs, look
up to Encounter twin orbs Etck of Adam Stone.*

'Hi,' *he says, as conductor regains dignity with
expression clearly registering regret that Page
Three-style Bimbette further up bus hadn't provided
similar opportunity.* 'I haven't met your friend.'

'Eff, orf, sunshine,' *proclaims bus conductor
artistically, disappearing upstairs in huff.*

I am speechless.

'Remember me? We met on the film course.'

*How could I forget? Is he really this modest?
Etck.*

'Every time I see you you make me glad I don't
have a baby brother.'

'Even this time?' *I stutter.*

'Well, I imagine that's his breakfast down your
front.'

*I always spill my cornflakes but I wasn't about
to admit that to A.S. Instead, we fell to relaxed
(YES!) chatter.*

*Chatter chatter we went as if we had known
each other for years. I decided I would miss my
stop and go wherever he was going but he
ruthlessly leapt up two stops before I was due to
get off. This was the parting of the ways, then.*

'You must come to the next lesson. Candice's
father's going to give us a talk. I know he makes

appalling films, but how can you resist?'

And, in a blur of blackberry curls and whirling limbs, Adam Stone was gone . . .

All day at skule I am taking advice, mostly from Aggy, but some from lesser mortals. I even consider asking Spiggy and am amazed and slightly shaken to find she is returning to Australia till half-term at least and maybe for ever! Something to do with a sick grandfather. She is V. Upset and I experience a microsecond of sympathy for her before recalling her betrayal of moi with Daniel. I don't ask how he's taking her departure but she tells me anyway: how he swears Undying Lurve till end of time and will be writing daily, visiting soon Etck Etck, bore bore. My heart is as Stone. Stone. Stooooooone. Adaaaaaam Stooooone. Swooooooooon.

Here is my train of thought, roughly:

a) **Glad to say** *Adam recognized me*
b) **Sad to say** *he saw me as pathetic victim of domestic strife, accident-prone luny, or (worse!) pitiful sekshul predator of bus conductors Etck*

a) **Glad to say** *he asked me to go to lesson*
b) **Sad to say** *reason for (a) was only to hear Candice's father speak. Note familiar use of 'Candice', who he obviously knows like back of gland Etck.*

a) **Glad to say** *that he thought Carthage senior made terrible movies* *b)* **Sad to say** *(a) prob means that he sees Candice as subtle & delicate flower that needs wresting from vicious & brutish Hollywood climate and rearing in tender fields of Art, Poetry Etck.*

However, must admit to being somewhat intrigued at idea of hearing Mogul Mogul Junior Third actually speaking in the flesh, not to menshun discovering whose flesh he's speaking into, arf arf. Maybe he cld get me Brad Pittbull's autograph? Also wld be a big star with Benjy's frendz Etck and they wld crowd round asking me secret of how the Rocket in Stradivarius IX *turned into a pirate ship Etck.*

Temptation beckons: urge to sup with Devil Etck. Might learn how to make mega-bucks or maybe other thing that rhymes with same, wld be definitely more interesting than Sleeve, shld forget Lurve to pursue career anyway and isn't werk a search for Lurve in another form after all? Etck Etck.

Decide to sleep on Big Decision, but BD out with someone else. Anyway, do not get much sleep as it happens, as return home to find message on newly installed ansaphone for my Only Mother from NEVILLE! Arg. The student she spurned for Father! Should I wipe the tape? Have just decided it is best course of action to save Only Mother from Her Self when she sweeps in and plays message with faint Mona Lisa type smile hovering at extremities of lips. Something about seeing her next weekend! Arg!

'Who's Neville?' innocently asks El Chubb, super-sleuth, newshound Etck.

'Just a friend' is her enigmatic and nerve-wrenching reply. I don't care how many second homes our Neville has got. I DO NOT want a step-father. Only Father suddenly seems the dearest person in werld. I make him cup of tea with a tea bag so strong the only reason you cannot stand the spoon up in it is because the spoon is decomposing too fast, just how he likes it, and tiptoe upstairs thinking how sad it is for him to have married a woman who likes china tea with lemon and is about to leave him for a poncey komputer salesman. I trip over Rover on stairs so Father only gets half a cup, but he is touchingly grateful none the less. To think he invested a fortune in the ansaphone so he could get messages about interviews Etck re his buke and the only call is from my Mother's fancy man! Should I tell him? But no, better to wait and see . . .

To add to my domestick Worries, Benjy claims there is a patch of carpet just by his bed that he doesn't like the look of AT ALL. He is convinced that after midnight it becomes a quicksand ready to swallow him up. Only Father claims he has taken up enough floor coverings to try to soothe Benjy's phobias and enough is enough. So marshmallow-hearted El Chubb to rescue yet again . . . I promise to come into Benjy's room after midnight and wake him up and stand on the patch to prove it is not a quicksand and he becomes completely hysterical.

'No Letto. Nonono Letttooooo. It will wallow you all UP!!!'

Are all families as mad as mine?

EARTH

This is all we got so we better look after it.
    See ENVIRONMENT.

EASTER

Easter is ye time for unbridled Chocolate Worship
which is V. Good news for Teenage Worriers and
OK for *moi* although I wld rather the eggs were
made of fudge. The reason we celebrate Easter

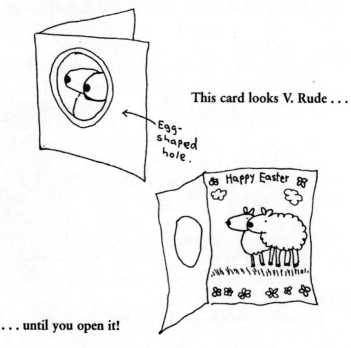

This card looks V. Rude . . .

Egg-shaped hole.

Happy Easter

. . . until you open it!

Sunday is that for Christians it is the day that Jesus rose From The Dead. This is a V. Cheery thought for those of us who hope for a LIFE After Banana, but does not explain how Easter Bunnies, egg-rolling Etck came into the picture. I used to think egg-rolling was about rolling the stone back from Jesus's tomb, but in fact it dates from Pagan times as it was part of the original celebration of Spring (ie: Spring equals New LIFE, so does an egg, so does Jesus's resurrection, so it all fits V. Neatly).

However, even the new Improved totally anti-diet El Chubb does panic at Easter. For the sight of Benjy and his chums overdosing on sticky heaps of eggies, bunnies, chocolate motorbikes Etck is not a pretty sight.

Last year we were up all night as after the Egg-hunt Benjy declared there were still several eggs hiding in his bed. Then he wept copiously because he had bitten the head off a chocolate teddy and thought the Teddy Police wld come for him and throw him into a dungeon with a hot chocolate floor. He fell into a fitful sleep complaining that his chocolate lawyer was demanding his pocket money for the next 500 years . . .

EATING DISORDERS

The main ones are Anorexia, where the sufferer starves, or Bulimia, where the sufferer binges and then throws up. (I have seen my Adored Father exhibit the latter symptoms, but I don't think he has Bulimia Nervosa, more like Alcoholia Ferocia.) They are common among young gymnasts and dancers, and Gurlz seem to suffer more than Boyz, but all kinds of people can get them. These illnesses can start quite gradually, with you just thinking you want to be thinner, or feeling V. Fussy about yr food. You can then get obsessed with the idea you are fat (wafer-thin anorexics feel like this!) and/or greedy. If you are bulimic you may sometimes eat huge amounts (sometimes as much as 30 times what you would normally eat) and then feel disgusted with yourself and make yourself sick. There are many complex reasons for this kind of misery and they are not ones you can disentangle on yr own. So if you think you are suffering from either of these disorders or you have a frend who is, it is V.V. Important to get help.

See also DIETS.

ECLIPSE

Rare occasions when moon blots out sun. This is how you feel when yr True Lurve leaves you for another. Your sun has gone out and all hope is eclipsed. If, however, you are lucky enough to have a beLURVed on Sep 23 2090, you may wish to watch the next total eclipse that will be visible from Britain. I have already written it in my hundred year diary, so that I can watch it with Adam Stone. I will only be in my early 100s by then, although we will probably only be able to see it from Land's End, or possibly even further out, but I'm sure Adam will still walk on water with or without a zimmer frame, and anyway it's even more romantic down in ancient mysterious Cornwall, full of Hobbits, hibbits, Bloggits Etck. I will be filming it, whether there is a man by my side or not.

EGG

What is an egg doing in an A—Z of LIFE? Will Men in White Coats remove El Chubb before end of buke? No, I put this in to remind you that this is where we come from and that Female Teenage Worriers produce an egg every month once they've started their periods. And that these little eggs, if they meet a squirmy sperm, can develop into miniature Worriers in a flash, though it akshully takes more than a flash to bring this state of affairs about, arf arf. So be warned! Keep Yr Eggs to Yrself until you feel you're good and ready, feel reasonably sure this event isn't going to undermine Yr hopes & Dreams, and pref V. Rich with large garden, servants, soundproof rooms for little *enfants* Etck.

See SEX.

ENGINEERING

This has usually been thought of as something only Boyz do, but recently things have started to change. Some Gurlz are becoming car designers, astronauts Etck, and have become V. Cross at the idea that widgets, sprockets Etck are things that only Boyz are interested in. This does of course lead to the possibility that Gurlz cld go on about these subjects

in just the same head-banging manner that some
Boyz do, which I'm not sure wld be a Good Thing.

Engineering is V. Imp in a technological society
like ours, because if Good Engineers don't make
things that are better for as many of us as possible,
Bad Engineers will make it a lot worse. However, be
warned. If you become an Engineer, you may have
to get yr Worrying under control. It's not much
good calculating the structure of the tallest building
on the planet if you're going to lie awake every
night waiting for the news that it's fallen down.

Campaign for more Gurl Engineers, Electricians
Etck. We can understand this stuff just as well as
Boyz. (NB: Thought of El Chubb: funny how
feminism tends to campaign for more Gurl
politicians, doctors, lawyers Etck but neglects
electricians, road sweepers Etck.)

ENVIRONMENT

Our planet is all we've got. So Teenage Worriers
had better Save It from Ozone destruction,
Deforestation, Vast piles of plastic, Nuclear
dumping, Extinction of species Etck Etck.

When I heard that most plastic couldn't be
recycled I panicked, I must admit. Look round yr
room at this very moment and see how much is
made of plastic.

In El Chubb's room:

Light fitting
Batman figures (why are Benjy's Batman figures always in my bed?)
Pens (26, only 2 working)
Pen tops (22, none of which match pens, above)
Walt Disney Ice Spectacular Mug (also eco-hazard since covered with unsavoury coat of green fur)
Fizzo bottle
Bubblo bottle

Puke-o bottle
Assorted tubs and tubes of glup
Horrible holiday sandals (the holiday was horrible
but the sandals are much worse)
Revolting hair slides
Combs (6)
Brushes (12 . . . guilt . . . why can I never find
one when I want it?)
Toy horses (for any Boyz reading – I got these
when I was 7)
Mini chest of drawers (must look inside – urg –
maybe not).
Strange roundish thing with wobbly bit
Cheapskate *Little Princess* bedhead (I thought
this was pukey even when I was 10 but attempts
to paint it ended in curious marbled effect which
I rather like now).
And so on and on. Benjy's room is much worse and
the kitchen is a disaster area. If this amount of
toxic waste exists in our humble home what hope
is there for entire planet?

EL CHUBB'S ENVIRONMENTAL TIPS:

* Look at aerosol cans to be sure they don't
  contain CFCs, which contribute to greenhouse
  effect, warming of earth so ice caps melt, ice
  cream melts even before you can eat it Etck.
* Dispose of rubbish in bins or take it home. My
  Adored Father verges on Road Rage when driving
  behind people who throw wrappers out of their

car windows, though shld the conflict come to court, it wld be as well the opposition lawyers shldn't see the room he works in.

* Join an environmental protection group like Greenpeace or Frenz of the Earth. Even the pittance you can spare them helps to challenge Big Bizness, Dodgy Govts Etck on damage to the planet that might make our lives as future Adults and parents V. Unhappy.

* Do not pick yr nose and wipe it under the desk. This is V. Damaging to skule eco-system, and possibly to Yr Own Personal Ego-System if discovered by Adored One who has previously put you on a pedestal Above All Others, some hopes, gripe, moan, whinge.

EUROPE

Geography has always been my V. Worst subject because I have geographical dyslexia, a rare medical condition invented, perfected, researched and suffered nobly by El Chubb. I know London is near the bottom of the British Isles and that Scotland is at the top and that Wales is on the left and that the whole lot looks like an old man with a beard. That's about it, but as we shamble towards European Union, linked to ye grate Outside Werld by Channel Tunnel Etck, I realize it is V. Imp to

understand the werkings of the Werld and therefore
to understand how we fit into it. Even more so
since all werk is becoming global now and money
leaps about the place electronically and Wicked
Financiers put it where people are prepared to slave
for 25 hours a day for one kopek Etck.

European dyslexia is a much more widespread
disease than Geog Dys (see above) and is suffered
by most of our politicians and nearly all citizens
over 30. They want to be on a nice little tight little
island and certainly don't want bossy foreigners
telling us that we should be giving blokes paternity
leave, or paying better pensions or other wimpy
things like that. I have V. Sneaky feeling that
Europhobia is about not wanting other folks to see
how stingy, poor Etck we are. On *le autre main*, as
they say in France, we need to preserve National
Culchur Etck as well as next nation. Yeeeeech. Olé!
Mon Dieu! Écu! Etck. I am going to werk V. Hard
to learn more about how it all werks.

EXAMS

Grue, yeech, screech, gnash Etck. Exams are
coming back in a big way in Our Soc, and Adored
Mother is V. Upset about the pressure it will put on
poor ickle Benjy having to sit SATs (if you follow
me) at the tender age of 7 Etck, when all she had

to do in skule at that age was occasionally splash a bit of paint over herself or act out a day in the life of an aardvark Etck, but then only if she really wanted to. I have realized from the only meagre few posh frendz I have (ie: Hazel, Hazel's brother and, once – sob – Daniel Hope) that getting into Oxford, Cambridge Etck is not simply a matter of yr native wit and brilliance (otherwise me, myself, *moi* would be there already of course, some hopes) but how determined yr teachers are to train you to do exactly what examiners want instead of Express Yrself. I have even heard of expensive cramming skules where the lessons are all different according to which entrance exam yr parents are putting you through, instead of Unfolding Vistas of Wondrous Knowledge about World Etck. Is this what Edukashun is for? I ask *moi*self.

But, however little they may reveal about YOU, the One True Person, exams are the way the system sorts out the people there might just be enough decent jobs for (and even this seems to be a fading hope) and you need to put some time and effort into them if you are not to end up in cardboard box, being dragged around by dog on piece of string Etck. Just dream of Riches Untold, World at Feet, washing in asses' milk Etck. By no means all of the people now living this lifestyle have been much good at exams, viz Royal Family, pop stars, footballers Etck, but since jobs of this kind are very few and far between, you need to narrow the odds on the ones that are left, ie: forget LIFE's joy for

one year for GCSEs and two years for 'A' levels.
See also SCHOOL.

EXERCISE

N.B. walk to school unless moving pavement, designed by El Chubb, (patent pending) is available near You.

If you're walking to skule and back, doing some sport and swimming (about half an hour three times a week in all) you should be getting enough exercise

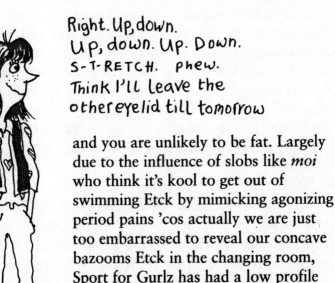

Right. Up, down. Up, down. Up. Down. S-T-RETCH. phew. Think I'll leave the other eyelid till tomorrow

and you are unlikely to be fat. Largely due to the influence of slobs like *moi* who think it's kool to get out of swimming Etck by mimicking agonizing period pains 'cos actually we are just too embarrassed to reveal our concave bazooms Etck in the changing room, Sport for Gurlz has had a low profile in the lives of Teenage Worriers.

Who WANTS to do a zillion sit-ups in three seconds; gallop through freezing mud and scratchy brambles (OK if you're on a horse); get kicked in shins chasing after ball with mind of its own or knocked unconscious by oaf with hockey stick? Us Kool Gurlz can think of better things to do, like varnishing our fingernails, peeling a grape and giggling in corners . . .

WELL . . .
that's what I used to think.

After my own dazzling skills at football went unremarked by teachers who discouraged Gurlz' teams (I'm glad to say this is one thing that's *beginning* to change . . .) I went into a sulk and found lifting the TV channel changer was about my exercise limit. But then along comes a lot of V. Convincing Evidence that exercise is good for you in lots of ways: not only does it keep you bouncy physically – and therefore less likely to suffer an early banana – but it also helps you concentrate, relax, feel happy and improves confidence.
Well well.

Obviously the above is not true of crazed Middle-aged Worriers who kit themselves out in fluorescent lycra to burn off calories on horrible-looking machines or let themselves be bullied by poisonal [*should that be 'personal'? – Ed.*] trainers.

El Chubb's version is: Lurve yr body enuf to take it for a brisk walk, refreshing dip in heated pool, frisky gambol with cat, dog Etck three or four times a week. Have supply of fudge handy to keep energy supplies up.

Campaign for equal sports facilities for gurlz

and boyz and don't be a wimp if you fall over, or lose. Games are supposed to be fun.

TYPICAL TEENAGE WORRIER'S EXERCISE REGIME:

7.10 a.m. Turn off alarm, pull pillow V. Sharply over head (exercises arms).

7.45 Shout back at parent that you have been up for hours. Shamble guiltily out of bed (whole bod, including lungs).

8.00–8.20 Usual masticating (this means chewing, you rude thing), scrubbing, flapping about stuff that gets some clothes on and food in bod.

Rest of day: skuley stuff. Pretend to have agonizing period cramps and so avoid any compulsory sport.

Evening: bits of masticating, shambling, flapping, as for morning. Some channel changing.

NB: Aerobics is where you keep moving enough to raise heart beat Etck for 20 minutes and is popular refuge of Middle-aged Worriers. OK if large quantity of fudge consumed between hours.

See also SPORT, WALKING.

EYESIGHT

Aggy first realized she needed glasses when she got on a bus to skule and ended up on a sightseeing

Middle

Distance

Reading

**Make a spectacle of yourself with L. Chubb's
REVOLVING SPECS-for-all-Reasons**

tour of the Changing of the Guard. She still didn't
go for an eye test, though, until about three of her
frendz had decided she was a stuck-up old bat
because she never said 'hello' to them in the street.
The final straw came when she failed to recognize
one of her aunties, who immediately started a Bad
Behaviour and Yoof of Today speech which sent
her chasing off to the Optician.

If you can't see bus numbers you are probably
short-sighted. If you can't read small print you are
probably long-sighted. Either way, it's best to get it
checked as you will be more of a social outcast if
you ignore your frendz, catch wrong buses, or can't
read the paper than you wld be in glasses. And you
can always save up for contact lenses later if you
really feel bad about having specs, although about
one in five teenagers need them, so it's not that
unusual. And in the humble opinion of El Chubb,
they look V. Interllekshual and Kool, especially

new designer frames Etck which some kids are now wearing with plain glass in them. Weird.

I always fancied Clark Kent more than Superman, myself, and Aggy's goggles, which really are V.V. Thick pebble-type glasses that remind you of little cottage windows or those dimpled beer mugs, certainly never put Daniel Hope off. Sigh . . . gnash. Maybe I shld get a fake pair to convince Adam Stone that although I may not have the allure of Ms Navel, I am instead a dashing interllekshual . . .

FAIRGROUNDS

Still El Chubb's big tip for a fun night out. I have always Lurved the tinkle of the Merry-go-round, the squeal of the ghost train, the dull thud of the wooden ball as it misses the coconut and hits yr ickle brother – even the sad little goldfish swimming round and round in their little plastic bags . . . Why is it, when I hate getting ripped off by manky advertisers, diet-mongers, cosmetics con-artists, I don't object to getting ripped off by Fairgrounds?

After all, you KNOW, when you try to get the ring over the pink panda, that it will never fit over the big wooden box that the panda is sitting on. You KNOW, when you fish with your little wooden stick for the plastic duck that it will NEVER be the duck that wins the LIFE-size toy gorilla . . .

But the great thing about the Fairground rip-off is that people who run fairgrounds are really *working* for it. They're driving around in caravans, unpacking enormous generators, putting up stalls, wiring up dodgems, cranking big wheel handles and shouting their heads off to convince you it's worth spending a quid on a ride.

Also, at any decent Fairground, you get something if you lose. Who cares if the fluffy toy is worth a quarter of what you paid to throw the darts? Benjy will still be thrilled with its little green face and furry claws.

FASHION

For the last year, what I facetiously refer to as my 'wardrobe' (ie, that is: three sweatshirts, three joggers, three T-Shirts) has always been in the following shades: sable, ebony, jet and fog. I am considering branching out into subtle shades of mist and cloud for Spring.

However, I always add my own personal touch, ie: waistcoat, jumper with hearts on, and make exception for pair of jeans. The outlay for this

Jumpers are what some Teenage Worriers wear when their Mothers feel cold

wardrobe, which suits all occasions, was £24.50 since everything but the jumper (knitted by Granny Chubb) came from charity shops.

Now hearken to me, any of you Kooltypes who think this sounds sad. Even ye grate Supermodels dress this way. They are so bored of the posh designer label type stuff they have to ponce about in all day for photographers that they like to relax in nice homey stuff that is Theirs Alone (even if it was someone else's before). More Imp, designer stuff goes out of Fashion V. Kwick, so if you want to avoid going out of Fashion take El Chubb's advice and never be IN Fashion in the first place.

Create ye Very Own Look. For some, it may be polka dot headscarves and frilly petticoats. For others, a beige tube, unadorned. Some may even like a little jumper for the face so that they can

look out at the werld without the werld always
looking in. little hats for ears may become a common
fancy. Or large green galoshes, resembling a frog.
Why not?

El Chubb sez there is a conspiracy of sameness
that tries to force penniless Teenage Worriers to
empty their pockets into the maw of the Fashion
Industry. Join El Chubb's Campaign against
Designer Labels! Or invent yr own.

See JEANS, TRAINERS.

FEDORA

V. Nice hat as worn by Humphrey Bogart in
Casablanca (one of the movies on your 'must-see'
list). Which wld suit Adam, I think.

FEELINGS

Feelings are supposed to be a V. Imp part of being
a Yuman Person, but when you're a Teenage
Worrier you can do with a few less of them,
because they seem to keep washing all over you
without warning and leave you standing there
bedraggled, confused and conspicuous.

But I know my Feelings for my Only Family

(speshally my Benjy), for Rover, Adam, my frendz, as well as my Feelings for ye poor, homeless, starving Etck are what go to make up El Chubb, and they're a way of knowing something about the Werld that I ought to trust as much as any other way of knowing or explaining things. If we lose our Feelings, then we might as well just get ourselves replaced by holograms, put ourselves away in deep-freezes, and save money in Food Etck.

On the other hand, if we are all Feelings and no Judgement, then we can't put ourselves in anyone else's place, which is what babies are like – and Adults who are like that often leave a lot of mess around for other people to clear up, just like babies do. So part of getting your Feelings sorted out is to remember that other people have them too. So protect your Feelings, Teenage Worriers, and they'll look after you!

FIRST AID

All Teenage Worriers shld have access to a V. Good First Aid Kit, ie: one containing slobs, sorry, swabs, loads of different plasters, bandages, antiseptic creams, anti-sting creams, scissors and preferably a V. Big Medical Dictionary . . .

But nothing beats going on a First Aid course, so I am told, and when I have overcome my V. Laziness

I am going to go on one (wish I had had the kind of sensible, pushy parents who made me go to Gurl Guides Etck so I wld have picked up these things when I was young).

The Red Cross and St John's Ambulance run V. Good courses so you can find out what to do if your sibling is choking on a marble and you might actually save a LIFE Etck.

FOOD

See DIETS and VEGETARIANISM.

FOOTBALL

A V. Odd thing happens to Boyz aged about 8 or 9. From complete ignorance of sport, overnight they know the names of all the Football players in the werld plus the scores of all the matches that have ever been played. This is proof that the Yuman brain is more powerful than the best komputer, as no one teaches them this stuff and none of these Boyz has ever been seen to read a buke! HOW does it happen? Boyz then go on to prove that Football is V. Much more interesting than Gurlz for the rest of their LIVES, eg: they will queue for hours in freezing rain to see it, spend all their dosh on related items, be over-moon when it goes their way and cry when it doesn't. When were they ever this moved by Lurve? If you can't beat 'em, join 'em, sez El Chubb. Or at least I did. I was V.V.V. Good at Football at my Primary Skule but they badly discouraged Gurlz from playing and it has left *moi* Scarred for LIFE. Campaign for Gurlz' Teams!! Campaign for Mixed Teams!! I am sure that in a few years' time we will be as good as Boyz at this. All it takes, after all, is Skill.

See also SPORT.

FREEDOM

'The condition of being free or unrestricted . . . personal or civic liberty; absence of slave status . . . the power of self-determination; independence of fate or necessity', the dictionary says. Freedom is a V. Complex thing, and it is V. Imp aspect of deciding what kind of World Teenage Worriers want to become Adult Worriers in. Frinstance, when the Cold War ended, bits of Berlin Wall turned into expensive souvenirs Etck, newspapers all said this was a Victory for Freedom, because people in Eastern Europe no longer had to Worry about being watched by secret police, told what job they had to do, denied opportunities to Travel World, wonder what it might be like to have Sky TV, Levi jeans Etck. I must say this does seem. V. Boring and Disagreeable way to live yr LIFE.

But now they all have Freedom, and many people in those parts of the Werld can't afford a loaf of bread any more while some are driving round in stretch limos Etck, so some are Freer than others. This is the kind of thing that can make yr Brain Hurt, but I think it's worth hurting it a bit for the sake of becoming Better Citizen.

I have a personal rule about Freedom, which is not a big new Lightbulb Above Wig thought, but which I try to keep reminding myself about. Treat other Worriers (and even non-Worriers, though LIFE is so much fairer to them they hardly deserve the break) as you wld wish to be treated Yrself. Freedom seems to go Down Plug when people stop thinking of other people as needing the same thingz they do.

FREEEEDOM'S JUST ANOTHER WORRD for nothing Left to LOSE

Old FolkSongs sometimes speakTRUE dept.

FRIDAY

Friday is a V. Confusing day in the anals, sorry annals, of El Chubb, because it is the last day of the skule week and therefore a Good Thing, but the beginning of the weekend, with all its potential for Worrying Events, non-Events Etck. It takes its name from Frigg (*with two 'g's – don't be rude*), or Friia, a character in Norse mythology, the wife of Odin and mother of somebody called Balder, and she can't have been much of a mother if she called – or allowed Odin to call – her son that in the first place. It's supposed to be a day celebrating marriage, love and byooty, so it's not surprising I have mixed feelings about it.

NB: other days of the week info to impress yr frendz: the days of the Sun, Moon and Saturn continue in Sunday, Monday and Saturday; the Anglo-Saxon name for Tyr, the Norse god of war, survives in Tiw's day (Tuesday); Odin or Woden's name continues in Wednesday; Thursday originates from Thor's-day, named in honour of Thor, the god of thunder.

SO, Worrier's Tips: wear sun-block on Sundays, Moon about on Mondays, fight on Tuesdays, wear wode on Wednesdays, wear rubber soles on Thursdays (in case of being hit by lightning).

FUDGE *slurp* *yum*

Fudge, Fu-u-u-dge. Fuuuuuurge. Say it loud and there's music playing. Say it soft and it's almost like praying. Etck.

If you are a genuine fudge aficionado you must score high in the following TRUE FUDGEFACTs QUIZ:

TRUE FUDGEFACTs QUIZ

1) What is the ideal flavour for fudge?
2) Describe the ultimate FUDGE texture.
3) When should you carry FUDGE?
4) Where should you carry it?
5) What is the best accompaniment to Fudge?
6) If you were a guest on Desert island Discs, what would your chosen luxury be?
7) If you had to choose between salad dressings, would you choose a)Thousand island b) French c)Blue cheese d)Grated fudge?
8) Have you ever made your own fudge?
9) How many kinds of fudge have you sampled?
10) Name ten things (not including people or pets) that you prefer to fudge.

FUDGEFACTS ANSWERS

1)FUDGE should be vanilla.

2) It should be soft with only a hint of crunch on the outer layers.

3)Always

4) Everywhere

5) More fudge

6) A lifetime's supply of fudge.

7) Grated fudge

8)To score a point, your answer should be "yes."

9) To score a point, you should be able to recall at least a dozen different fudges in detail

10) if you can name ten (or even four) things you prefer to fudge, I'm afraid you cannot join L.Chubb's Fudge de Luxe Club.

A score of Ten entitles you to fully paid up membership, plus *Fudge de luxe* badge, certificate, recipe buke Etck. Just make a cheque for £159.99 payable to El Chubb Enterprises Ltd. and await your gorgeous package.

CHAPTER SIX
GEEEEZE, HHHHHHHEZZ
AND IIIIIIZE

*Deciding factor about going to film lesson has been
to assuage Benjy's misery at losing his Year One
skule work, which of course I left behind at the class
in my abject confusion and hot desire to escape. My
Mother was distraught about it since it contained a
Mother's Day card with about 8 zillion kisses on it
and 'I lov you biger than a cake' V. painstakingly
inscribed upside down within. I admit that this is a
thing worth keeping but I am V. Frosty with my
Mother just now (not that she notices) and am more
influenced by the pitiful cries of dear Benjy, Viz:*

*'S'got my stickers innit. And my pictures of a
War machine for cutting baddies heads off and then
torcherin' the bodies till they confess.' Oh well.*

*Secretly think I might get chance to show my
moving photographs at last, and win Adam's
affections away from the dread Candice. But this is
a slim hope, since whole class will be agog at the
star performance.*

*Five gurlz I hardly know at skule have given me
their autograph bukes to take to Mogul and I am*

*V. Embarrassed but feel it my duty to try, and more
importantly they will go round saying I made it all
up if I don't . . .*

*Go home from skule early and try on 5 tops,
all of them different shades of black. Decide on
darkest, plus fog-coloured trousers as on first day,
as they are only pair I have without scorch marks.*

Quake off to lesson.

*Mogul Mogul Junior Third is a vast slab of a
man with voice like motorbike engine, oozing
power, wit, charm, danger Etck and leering at
entire class who he obviously expects to fall into
bed with him at flash of gold tooth, dentist's bills
Etck. Makes particular eyes, I feel, at Adam, as it
happens.*

*Tells us all about how he was born in shoe box
at bottom of municipal garbage tip Etck and
struggled to feed his crippled sister on pieces of
used takeaway fried chicken boxes Etck, eking a
living by selling fictional maps of Hollywood stars'
favourite nude bathing locations to tourists from
Tennessee. Whilst in intensive care following one
such transaction, Mogul received delirious vision of
man spirited away by space aliens for experiments,
condemned to repeatedly returning to earth as
chicken nugget, vainly attempting to proclaim his
difference from all the rest before asphyxiation by
barbecue ketchup and descent into bowels of
gruesome winos Etck. Provides theme for first
great Mogul work,* Close Encounters of the Slurred
Kind. *Know he has made this bit up and that most*

*of audience hasn't realized, so am beginning to like
him when he skips 20 years and, glancing at his
watch, tells us exactly how much each of his films
has grossed at box office. My writing hand now V.
Numb at adding loads of 000000000000s to every
figure he mentions and then doubling them.*

Suddenly it's over.

*'Any questions?' He can barely conceal his
impatience.*

'Does your sister like your films?' I bravely jibber.

*'Never asked her.' He laughs a scornful laugh
exactly like a villain in a horror movie, as if to
teach us that scraping yourself up to top of ladder
from V. Humble beginning does not necessarily
make you a Nice Person. He sweeps out with
Candice under his giant, batlike wing. Everyone else
sweeps after him, waving autograph books. Sleeve
is quivering with fulfilment. No sign of Adam.*

All is lost.

A hand on my arm. 'Let's get out of here.'

*I turn to gaze into twin orbs, coal dark with
twinkling fires in depths. Etck.*

*'He was even worse than I thought,' laughs
Adam, dazzlingly. Swooooon.*

Adam Stone and I GO FOR A COFFEE.

*We talk for two hours about Art, Poetry, the
Mysteries of the Yuniverse, Etck. Adam cares
nought for power or money, but only how to forge
a Better Werld Etck. He Lurves my photographs!*

*Most amazing of all, he has asked me to go to
Large Door with him tomorrow night!!!! It is*

apparently a V. Grate black and white movie
of the kind Adam and I (how easily that little
couplet tinkles on my tongue) Lurve. I have found
a soul mate! As we part, he gently squeezes my
hand, a light brush of flame, a millisecond of
Perfect Bliss.

Luckily, tomorrow is Friday and I am allowed
to go out with Aggy. I can easily put her off and
sneak to cinema without embarrassing questions
from nosy parents. My cup runneth over. I float
on wings of pashione Etck.

GAMBLING

A V. Bad thing, say the Fingerwaggers in Authority.
The way to a life in a cardboard box, or even a
wooden box.

And we are all encouraged to do it. From that
first crisp packet that says 'Win £200 if you can find
a blue crisp inside', all the way up to the National
Lottery which makes people believe they have a
chance of winning gazillions, and lets Govt off hook
re funding stuff it thinks is trivial, like The Artz.

I wouldn't mind all this hypocrisy from the
Adult Werld if

a) People weren't spending more than they can
really afford of their Benefit on the Lottery and

b) Winning 8 million quid made people feel happier, which to judge by newspaper stories of families falling out, winners going mad Etck it doesn't always seem to.
  See MONEY.

All moi needs is an Ace of Hearts (sigh)

GARDENS

Gardening is the favourite pursuit of Middle-aged Worriers. If they can't stumble around with an old trowel in a silly-looking hat, then they will listen to V. Old people with lurching country accents burbling about it on the radio. But getting your mitts stuck in the earth is V. Good for soul whatever your age, and for sheer entertainment I dare you to listen to a Gardening programme on the radio. (Yes! Radical!) Far from being quiet, purring programmes, everyone always disagrees with each other: a little old lady from Godalming will ask what the best treatment for her wilting *Rosaria lavabo* is and . . .

Dr Pete Bogg will insist she needs more acid in her soil and a sprinkling of rotten cow bones every second Tuesday. He will be contradicted by Crumbilia Barke, with a sturdy assertion that *Rosaria lavabo* must never be treated with anything on Tuesdays and that it needs considerably less, rather than more acid. In wades Farmer Slurry, robustly denying everything that has gone before and saying that his favourite plant is the *Rosaria lavabo*, a Thing of Byooty and a Joy For Ever: he had one growing outside his only windowsill when he was a young boy without shoes or toes in the West Country and what he loved most was the smell of the Rosario lavabo as it wafted up through the cow dung of a Summer's Morn . . . We move on to Professor Thorn, who briskly says he loathes the *Rosaria lavabo*, doesn't think it's worth growing, especially in Godalming where the soil is too earthy. Also, he feels that cow bones are spreading BSE causing Mad Plant Disease, in which cucumbers think they're personal vibrators and turn pink. He would grow a nice cactus instead and can recommend several varieties. Instead of

leaving in a huff, the sweet little old lady from
Godalming thanks them kindly and goes home to
her beloved *Rosaria lavabo* none the wiser, but
replete with the satisfaction of having her question
addressed by the experts.

There are two important LIFE-Skills here for the
Teenage Worrier:

1) You don't have to know the answers, you just
have to SOUND as if you do.
2) Regional accents are an advantage in
Gardening Experts.

However, LIFE can be enhanced by Gardens:
planting runner beans, frinstance, is V. Rewarding.
You get seeds (qu. Cheap) which just look like dried
beans and all you do is push them in a bit of earth in
the Spring. The result is amazing – like Jack and the
Beanstalk they just run right up the little bamboo
poles you have also stuck near the seeds and soon
they have red flowers and then they have beans!
Lots! You only need a teensy patch of earth for this.

GAY

If you prefer same SEX to opposite SEX you are
like most folk on planet. BUT, if you like your own
SEX in a sekshual way, you may find you are
prone to Worry, since this is considered by ye grate

unwashed public as not quite NORMAL. Since V. Little that I do (ie: praying in public highways, bending down to touch floor at odd moments, turning lights on and off twice) is also considered not normal I have much empathy. But in my view being Gay is just like being anything else. It's part of who you are and the world is slowly but happily coming to realize this. If you are lonesome though, you need mates who are also Gay. If you can't find any easily, join a group, ring a helpline Etck.

GERBIL

Horace's cousin.

Sweet-looking, inoffensive (except in case of Horace) pet who will do if you can't afford horse or dog. Like hamsters they enjoy running round on wheels and shredding stuff.

GONDOLA

No Dream of LIFE is complete without a trip on a gondola up the canals of Venice singing one cornetto. Venice will prob have sunk without trace by the time I have enough dosh to afford this. I wonder if Adam's folks are rich? (Although of course I wld Lurve him anyway, Etck.)

GRAMMAR

Grammar is a boring waste of time people say its
v imp to learn speling punctuation past participles
adjectives nouns adverbs sentences paragraphs
and all those tedious things because if you dont
you wont be able to get a job b keep a job c make
yourself understood d feel like the intelligent
worthwhile person you are e get LIFE skills to
enable you to make sense of what youre reading
now or anything else and also although its often v
boring at the time it does make you think that all
the people who invented this rich and wonderful
language of ours which is all of us over several
centuries by the way are v clever and it would be
a pity to let it all go down the plug because we
cant be bothered to learn a few rules about full
stops sometimes I would like it if my teachers
didnt scribble all over my werk correcting it all
the time so that I could just go with the flow I
am now wondering whether the time has come
to end this ramble since it is v tiring not putting
in any punctuation I am surprised to find its
easier to do it the right way I think I have learned
an important LIFE skill and instead of moaning
I will try v hard to be a better person etck etck
moan whinge by the time I have finished this
buke I will be a boring old f--- who thinks
everyone should dot their is and all that old
rubbidge

GUILT ,worry, worry, guilt, worry ....

Teenage Worriers are prone to Guilt because as well as Worrying about all the terrible thingz that might happen to us, we Worry about all the terrible thingz that might happen to everyone else, which we believe we've caused by being too lazy/selfish/ignorant/demanding/indifferent to Fate of Werld Etck. Viz: 'If I had given 50p to Frendz of the Earth instead of spending it on fudge another whale wld be alive today' . . . 'If I had given Benjy a second piece of fudge he wld not have run out of back door in huff, and thus avoided treading on rake and whacking head' Etck.

LIFE-Advice about Guilt is that LIFE isn't perfect and therefore people won't be Happy, free from disasters, bad news Etck all the time, so there's no point in feeling Guilty about yr failures to prevent something that might have happened anyway.

Guilt does exist for a reason, though, because it is part of our CONSCIENCE and a Conscience is a vital part of being a Yuman Bean, stopping us doing bad thingz or helping us put them right.

HABITS twitch... tic.... gulp

Habits and Worriers often go hand in hand, and sometimes they couldn't be prised apart with a crowbar. Habits are, of course, thingz that you do repeatedly, and you may be aware of them or not. Some Habits are OK, because they look Kool. Other Habits are not Kool, like praying all the time in public and hoping people don't notice, picking your nose whilst sharing candlelit dinner with Person of yr Dreamz, eating chips out of newspapers while snogging Etck. (Though V. Trashy Habits *can* become Kool with the right people, Garage music, Grunge fashions, Trainspotting-type lifestyle Etck).

Get a Grip on Yr Habits! I wish I cld, but I still

1) Twiddle my fringe
2) Touch things twice
3) Always keep my lucky rabbit's foot in my pocket
Etck.

Hanging on to these Habits a bit longer helps to keep me sane, I *think*.
See also PHOBIAS.

HANDWRITING

My handwriting looks like the printouts from an earthquake seismograph being used on a toboggan, and I wish I'd concentrated more on ps and qs at Primary Skule. It's hard to get better at the ancient age of 15 and I think it's V. Unfair that we all have to write job applications in our own writing as people like *moi* will be thought unintelligent when really we're just lazy (ahem) – I mean suffering, um, co-ordination problems or left/right brain probs. Actually, this IS really mean if you are dyslexic but in my case I just didn't bother. It will be a lot easier for Benjy's generation as everyone will just be emailing their life histories and they won't have to use a pen at all.

**Pre-teen-Worrier's handwriting
on starting Secondary Skule**

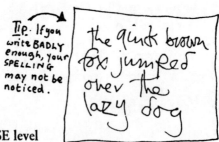

. . . and at GCSE level

For LIFE-Tricks today, however, I urge you to try and enjoy it by getting an italic pen. This was the most boring present I had last Christmas but,

to my surprise, I started enjoying it in Feb when
I had the flu and *TeleTubbies* was over (I was
watching it with Benjy, ahem) and I got it out and
started doodling. And it was FUN. I even made a
V. Good looking Treasure Map (for Benjy, blush)
that looked like it was written by an Ancient
Hand. Unfortunately we set light to the furniture
shortly after, in attempting to make the map go all
brown and parchmenty, but that's another story . . .

HANGING OUT
(aka Hanging About In The Street)

Essential LIFE-Skill for Teenage Worriers, deprived
of dosh and the chance to make any, is to Hang
Around on Street Corners. Whether you decide to
Look Threatening or not is down to whether or
not you want to:

a) Worry old ladies.
b) Worry Teenage Worriers like *moi*self, who
will walk three blocks to avoid a large gang of
yelling yoofs who might be qu. Harmless.
c) Get moved on by The Bill.

To avoid above means hanging around in
smallish groups, with hyena-like smile affixed to
yr mug (rather than jackal-type scowl which is

common face-in-repose mode). It's a V. Cheap way to have fun. You can:

a) Watch the local talent (no rude remarks per-*lease*).

b) Amaze yrself at variety of yumankind that wanders down average street. Viz: Man with carrier bag on head; V. Tall person of ambiguous gender dragging poodle on string; roller-blading pensioner. And the *clothes*: You couldn't make them up. You think most people have trousers and shirts or dresses on, don't you? Look again.

c) Oh well. How about just, er, talk?

HERMAPHRODITE

What a lot of Teenage Worriers think they might be (ie: neither man nor woman). Gurlz Worry about this if they have hairy chests, deep voices, no periods Etck. Boyz worry if they have high voices, titchy willies, some bazooms Etck. Real Hermaphrodites (the word comes from the union in one body of Hermes and Aphrodite) are V. rare, but it is poss to have hormone imbalances, so if you are worried about any of the above (or other things I have not thought of, like an unconquerable urge to grow a beard, even though you are a gurl) then talk to your doc about it. Hormone imbalances can usually be quite easily redressed and it is worth keeping an eye out, just in case.

BUT it is clearly a Big prob for your general LIFE-Skills stuff if you don't know which sex you are, or you think you want to be the one you are not. It MIGHT be a good idea if you cld find this sort of stuff out before you had a family . . . or became a Catholic Priest or something so you could avoid headlines like FROCK SHOCKS FLOCK. Arg.

HOBBIES

The most imp thingz you can do in LIFE are the things you enjoy. This is one thing many Adult Worriers have forgotten, but it is worth pointing out that men seem better at it than women. Here is an eg of a Sunday morning: Blokes are off to football, or cricket, pottering in sheds, fussing about with fish hooks, sawing up little bits of wood, tinkering with pieces of car Etck Etck. Or maybe watching blokes doing any of these things on TV.

Women are flaffing about with saucepans, irons, dusters Etck, nagging blokes and kids about old socks, fluff Etck. Who is enjoying themselves the most?

I am ashamed to describe this scenario as I am a feminist Etck but it does seem to me that blokes have a better time and not just because they leave all the boring stuff to the women and it's unfair but because they know how to enjoy themselves without feeling guilt (see GUILT).

Even as a young (ahem) teenager, I noticed that there was SOMETHING MISSING from my life that was not missing from BOYZ' lives: they were messing about with plastic model kits constructing giant aeroplanes or involving themselves in huge battlefields populated by miniscule warriors with names like Orko the Dread, or, if *they* weren't out chasing a ball they were at home playing miniature version called SOCKO, HOCKO or CRICKO. It was about this time that we Gurlz started putting away childish things and Worrying. We started to Worry about clothes, Worry about Hair, Worry about Boyz. Arg.

If you have a Hobby, you have El Chubb LIFE-Tricks award-winning potential, which means possible route to happiness.

There are Hobbies and pursuits you do with other people (like Music, Drama Etck – see rest of buke) or there are Hobbies you do on yr own. These are V. Imp for internal serenity Etck and include:

READING

V. Brilliant, as you can have conversations with the author as well as the characters.

Role-reversal brought on by reading

Advantages: V. Cheap. In fact, free as long as you get the bukes back to the library on time. Also, you can enter other werlds Etck and this is V. Good for the Soul if the werld you're in is a glume-laden battlefield of divorcing parents, exam-terror, heartbreak or whatever. With a good buke you can forget everything – while you're reading.

Disadvantages: people can get V. Snotty about bukes. I read recently of one mother who said she would only get her son horror books if he read one in French(!) for every one he read in English . . . I wonder if he's still reading anything at all. Middle-class parents seem to think Enid Blyton or the *Beano* are somehow bad for kids. V. Weird. If I hadn't cut my teeth on the *Beano* I don't think I would have ever got round to Dickens Etck.

Also, teachers and skule can be V. Good but can also help wreck books by looking at them too closely and spoiling the Dream. The Dream is a V. Imp part of the process . . .

DRAWING

Best of all for *moi* as you can literally make any-thing happen. Most kids draw all the time until they are about 9. Then someone laughs at a pic-ture, or they look at a photograph and see it looks different or some idiot tells them they can't draw and whoop, zammy! Away it goes. And with it a lifetime's pleasure.

Drawing should be for fun, not to be a brilliant artist. It really is a hoot making up characters, inventing daft situations, doing squiggles and turning them into objects Etck. Sort of doodling-with-a-bit-more-purpose. There are lots of famous cartoonists who don't draw 'well' in an Art Skule kind of way, but they have a great sense of huy-mour and somehow that squiggles into the line and – bingo!

Advantages: Cheap – most people can get hold of pencils and paper. Gets expensive if you start graduating to oil paint – but who needs that? This is Hobby time. NB: A V. Simple child's watercolour box lasts for ages and you can get loads of good effects.

Disadvantages: Snottiness as above only along the lines of 'Why don't you do a Still Life, instead of those stupid comic book copies?' To which I reply, 'It may not be Art, but it's still LIFE.'

Adults often think you're wasting time. Being Happy is NOT a waste of time, they're just jealous.

WRITING

Exactly the same as drawing, above. Stories, poems Etck can really help you feel better and also keeping a Dairy is V. Good way of venting rage against Werld Etck.

MAKING STUFF

This can be anything from clothes to sculpture. My own tragick attempts at making trousers last year did nothing for my fashion self-esteem, ditto my attempt at knitting under the patient tutelage of Granny Chubb, than whom there can never have been a better teacher. Even she had to admit that the knotted, multicoloured, fluff-encrusted tube that resulted was more holey than a Gruyère cheese and could not pass as a scarf that even Benjy would agree to plonk under his chin. However, many Teenage Worriers of a more domestic turn of mind like perfect Hazel can run up dazzling little numbers out of bin bags, old sacks, loo rolls Etck and pass themselves off as Supermodels wearing the latest Designer togs without batting an eyelid. And they enjoy it.

The stuff I like making is sculpture from Found Objects. This requires lots of patience but a minimum of co-ordination as you can stick anything to anything really. Beach-combing is good for this. Old starfish are a good find, so are shells and bobbly seaweed. But what I really like is driftwood that has been bleached and rubbed by the elements Etck. You can make great mobiles with this (must see if I can get a job as a crafts writer on *Adorable Adobis* magazine – puke). Benjy does a lot of Found Object stuff: loo rolls, egg boxes, that sort of thing, all decorated with bits of old wool and milk bottle tops then left to rot on the kitchen table as my Mother is too sentimental to ever throw them away . . .

Advantages: V. Cheap. All you have to buy is glue (not always that easy as newsagents round here hardly stock any strong stuff 'cos so many Teenage Worriers are tragickly solving their Lack-of-Hobby-Situation by getting into a Solvent-Abuse-Situation).

Disadvantages: You need space. Not available to *moi*, sadly. Last week I had to throw out my beautiful Serpent Tempting Adam (ahem), which was made of a bicycle wheel and 12 old paint tins.

COLLECTING

If you enjoy collecting stuff, it gives you an identity that makes it V. Easy for people to choose your presents. Viz: 'Oh, that's old Mary, we can give her another frog, Dalmatian, egg cup, or whatever.'

Also, a V. Good talking-point for frendz 'Cor! What a lot of Dalmatians. Where DID you get them all? That one's as big as a hippo. And is this little chap made of glass? How clever – whoops! Only one of its kind? Flown all the way from Outer Mongolia? SO sorry.'

Advantages: Obsessively interesting to the collector: wherever they are they're on the lookout and never bored. Means frendz think of you whenever they see the object you collect. Could be good for reminding Lurvers of your existence, or even keeping job in later LIFE. 'We can't chuck poor Francilla out of her office!

Equipment for Making Stuff

1) GLUE (or chewing gum)
2) PAPER (only father's novel)
3) TISSUES, LOO PAPER ETCK.
(pref unused, this is a family buke)
4) OLD EGGS (plus boxes)
5) BITS OF FLUFF
6) GRAVEL
7) BIG BIT OF CARD or WOOD (I used table, but had to cut legs off. Benjy now starving as refuses to eat breakfast off floor, like rest of us)
8 PAINT
9 NICE BITS AND PIECES

INSTRUCTIONS

Cover 7 with 1. If using gum, chew well, then dot liberally over surface. Rip up 3 and stick to 7. Add more 1. Chuck handfuls of 5 and 6 at 1. Add 4 and 3. Decorate with 8 and 9.

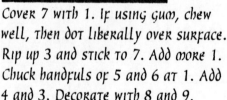

Turner Prize within my grasp . . .

Think how much we'd miss her tea cosy collection.'

Disadvantages: Could be V. Boring for other people. They are trying to enjoy film, while Collector-Person wants to rewind video to catch another glimpse of penguin, priceless jug or whatever. Expensive. Could be disadvantage for later LIFE-skills. 'Either Francilla goes, or her tea-cosy collection does.'

See also ART, DRAMA, MUSIC, RAINY DAYS.

HOMEWORK

The first, deeply harrowing truth about Homework is that it has to be done. You cld, as happens in boarding schools, do ye Homework immediately after lessons so it's just like a longer skule day, but most people like to feel skule days don't go on for ever, so you have to find a way of making yrself do it later, which is V. Hard.

But if you don't, you may feel V. Bad about yrself, if you are truly a Teenage Worrier and not the kind of person who says 'Stuffit' about anything they don't like, and doesn't mind being moaned at all the time.

Why do you feel Bad? Because having your parents/carers/Irresponsible Adults on your back every night is painful and glumey for all concerned.

Fact: Kids in Care often don't do homework. That's because there's often nobody around with the time or involvement in them personally to make them.

Result: These kids do not do so well at skule, and feel rejected all the more even if they act tough and say it's all krap anyway. It's not because they can't; it's just that no one is helping out.

Good teachers are also V. Good incentives for Homework, because if they make the subject interesting, you want to show them you think it is too. Unfortunately, this is not as common an incentive to do homework as we might like.

There are loads of ways to do Homework, but I've narrowed them down to three basic models – and only one will cure nagging Homework Worry (leading to glume, dume Etck).

MODEL 1

Get home without Hanging Out (see p. 149). Do Homework in dazzling firework display of Creative Genius, Brilliant New Ideas Etck. Reward self after with dazzling firework display of Wild Fun, stunning frendz with scintillating wit, Werld Knowledge Etck. Best option if poss but V. Uncommon.

MODEL 2

Get Home. Have snack/watch TV/pick nose. Think about Homework. Go out. Come back (as Homework Worry prevented you enjoying outing). Worry about Homework. Have meal. Watch TV. Worry a lot about Homework.

Fall asleep. Wake up V. Miserable.

Do Homework in mop cupboard or on loo first thing in morning, so no one can see you, but cause general household chaos in second case as everyone is banging on the door. Resulting work wobbly and somewhat stained.

MODEL 3
Get Home. Have snack. Start Homework. Get diverted by frend, TV programme, enormous emerging pluke bursting through walls of hooter and burying surrounding family in Pompeii-like molten swamp Etck. Follow Model 2 above but for longer and later. Wake up too late and tired to do Homework. But at least you started it, you say to yourself as you wander ashy faced to glumey skule and try to hide from enraged teacher for day.

HORSES

Most noble of beasts, but owning one – and even getting to ride one – is sadly out of reach of yr average Urban Teenage Worrier. Riding lessons are V.V.V.V. Expensive but you can get them by offering to help out at stables or saving a whole year's pocket money for about three lessons Etck. I have been riding four times with Hazel and they have been happiest times of LIFE (sob). Why? I think it's to do with freedom, soul in harmony with beast and nature, wind in hair, all that sort of stuff. And, since Hazel lent me hat, I did not even suffer falling-off terror that you would expect from nachural-born Worrier.

LIFE-long Dream of L. Chubb to own horse currently reduced to proprietorship of four rubber, two plastic, three china and one fake fur model arranged in shambolic cluster on bookshelf above bed. Many hours grooming their ickle manes, making saddles, rugs Etck out of felt and tacky off-cuts of leather have not helped yrs Truely to overcome her Urge. One day, I WILL have that palomino stallion prancing boldly in my meadow . . .

IMAGE

Feeling bad about yr image? Join El Chubb's

Teenage Worriers before and after positive thinking
NB: proof that poetry is oft based on PAIN ..

Frolicsome Feelgood Group. And take the
following Hints and Tips:

Stand in front of a mirror. Describe yourself out
loud or write it down, just as though you were
describing a sunset, or a building or a bowl of
fruit. (OK I know I look like an eclipse, a sky
scraper, a squashed banana – help, bananas are
now making me think about that word about dying
that rhymes with 'breath' – but that's just 'cos I'm
in a negative mood.) Let's think positive (sweat,
grone, massive circulation increase of bluddle to
single brain-cell Etck). If you don't like something
you see, ask yourself why?

So you think you've got a fat nose? Truly? How
fat? Who said so? Are they right? How fat is *their*

nose? What has *your* nose got to do with them anyway?

Next time you do this, list all the things you like about yourself. There should be just as many (how about that 48th hair just above yr left eyebrow? Or that really nice lone eyelash?). Feel pleased about that eyelash. No one else will, and it needs all the Lurve it can get. If it's the only thing you liked, then ask yrself why?

'Live happily in your body' say the advice bukes. Well, let's not be cynical for a minute (OK, for a second). It is poss to feel as though your body is fun – and not just a ramshackle contraption of bits and pieces that have been nailed together anyhow and attached to your soul whether you like it or not.

Good ways of getting 'in touch' (puke) with the 'whole you' (yuk) are exercises that use all your bits, like swimming and yogurt – sorry, yoga – and nice kinds of free zappy dancing (not twiddling around on points and worrying what you look like).

Ever noticed that sporty people are often the most confident? El Chubb thinx (and eggsperts agree) that this is 'cos running about a lot makes lots of little endorphins charge about and these, in their turn, cheer you up. Being fit(ish) means being happy(ish). Getting obsessed with being fit (like all obsessions – sigh) makes you sad. Arg. Must peel self off sofa and exercise ears with gentle flapping before hurling spindly frame into foam bath.

INITIATIVE

You need to show plenty of this to get on in
Wicked Cruel Werld. An eg of Lack of Initiative
wld be:

Parent: 'What is that strange aroma like boiled
plastic?'
Teenage Worrier: 'I think it is the aroma of
burnt plastic, perhaps mixed with a hint of scalded
milk.'
Parent: 'Where the F***'s it coming from?'
Teenage Worrier: 'I believe it's emanating from
the kitchen.'
Parent: 'What the **** is it?'
Teenage Worrier: 'It seems that the milk
saucepan's burnt dry and is now melting.'
Parent: 'Why the **** didn't you turn off the
gas?!!!!'
Teenage Worrier: 'Ummmmmmm.'

If you want a teeny chance of getting a job do
not be like the Teenage Worrier above (or the
parent, either, who should have rushed to stove
armed with fire blanket, extinguisher Etck instead
of maundering on asking stupid questions and
using werds which they would prefer you didn't
use yourself). Initiative is obv V. Imp to secure
place in labour market Etck.
    See JOBS.

INSOMNIA

Trouble sleeping usually means that an average
Teenage Worrier is more Worried than usual (or
that their ickle brother has had another nightmare
re the floor turning into used loo paper Etck).
Worry can be caused by over-excitement in
Teenagers just as much as in small kids. Even a
scary film can do it, or meeting a Lurve-object.

Usual old stuff like warm drinks is best remedy,
plus reading V. Old, comforting buke (like *A Pony
for Patsy*, which can either make you feel V. Cosy
and back on Adored Mother's knee, or so overcome
by boredom that you fall asleep in self-defence).
Counting sheep always fails for *moi* as I start to get
sorry for them all jumping over a gate and then I
imagine them jumping over a hedge; then I get
interested in how high they can jump and start
Worrying whether they will break their legs Etck.

If all these fail and you haven't slept properly for
a couple of weeks and have examined your soul for
reasons, then it's a good opp to go to doc and pour
yr heart out. My doctor always grones audibly at
the sight of *moi* in waiting room as she is used to
me turning up for brain tumours Etck when I have
just been wearing too small a hat, or fatal illnesses
that most people wld recognize as the common
cold. But Insomnia could be due to some quite
deep glume and if you are deeply glumey good
doctors shld be V. Sympathetic.

INTELLIGENCE

Ours is a Cruel Werld that rates children by IQ tests, crazed exam results, how early they do joined-up writing Etck Etck and neglects Whole Person.

Pause, sez El Chubb, and ask yourself, 'What is Intelligence?' Is it that which distinguishes (if that's the right werd) us from the animals?

Is it virtue?

Can it be measured?

If so, how can the people with lots of it be encouraged to benefit the rest of us rather than just use it to get rich?

Whether you think you have much of this elusive quality or not, it's clear that it comes in many versions. There's the obvious kind that gets four A* grades at 'A' level and a scholarship to Oxbridge. This kind, however, is often nurtured at the hands of expensive schools and tutors and may lie dormant in the child of a household none of whose members have ever seen the inside of a book.

Then there's the creative kind – that is, good at

Spot the Teenage Worrier with the highest IQ

painting, or music, or inventing. This, too, can be encouraged or crushed by environment. Everyone can learn to play a musical instrument quite competently, frinstance, but most of us never get taught.

Then there's intuitive Intelligence: that's people who are really good at people-thingz, like understanding, consoling, energizing.

Then there's the enquiring kind, full of mad professors and wild psychiatrists. We need these especially for the Teenage Think Tank.

Then there's practical Intelligence – those amazing foks who seem to have been born knowing how to get FM radio on a hairdrier with the addition of a few everyday household utensils.

There is also a growing area of Intelligence to do with survival in The Street – which involves V. Quick assessment of developing situations, ability to change mindsets V. Fast Etck.

I am still trying to discover which, if any, of these Intelligences I possess and so far I have not exhibited the Intelligence to decide. But what I DO know is that developing as many of them as possible is a surer route to Happiness, Fulfilment Etck than developing your body/personality/looks.

Imagine what the articles in *Smirk* COULD look like . . .

Incredible fact: Even if you fed 10 pieces of new information into your brain every second you still wouldn't ever fill it up (not even HALF-full) in your whole LIFEtime. The Totally Free Yuman Brain is some awesome komputer.

CHAPTER SEVEN
JJJJJZE TO LLLLLLLZE

*Awake on wings of desire Etck in Lurve with whole
werld. Werk V. Hard at skule. If only teachers knew
how subtle are the yearnings of a Teenage Worrier
and that the happier you are, the better you work.
Um, not sure this is always true as mooning, moping,
day-dreaming Etck are fave habits of Teenage
Worriers-in-Lurve. Nevertheless feel V.V.V. Positive.*

*Get flowers for Granny Chubb on way home,
no expense spared etck. Welcomes bunch of V.
Classy roses as 'Lovely daisies', but I am not to be
deterred from Positive Mood today, even if she had
said they were bunch of miserable weeds she wld
not give table-room to Etck.*

*Make firmer resolution to step up GCSE
endeavour and work out ways of earning dosh,
though suspect Mogul Mogul did not take GCSEs.
Film-directing may not immediately be as lucrative
as I had hoped, especially if I follow the dictates of
my soul Etck and concentrate on Deep and
Meaningful projects involving Angst, long silences,
sounds of people making Lurve while camera
tracks across Inner City wasteland of dustbins,
dead cats (akshully Rover asleep), abandoned sick*

aunts Etck rather than falling for gloss and glamour
of Big Bucks Productions Inc.

Register faintest tremor of disappointment at this
momentous realization, but impelled to soldier on
nevertheless to new dawn of righteousness (hopefully
marching side by side with Adam Stone, swoooon).
Fix up Hazel's video camera on complicated timing
mechanism, so that it will film Urban Dekay outside
my window at craftily timed intervals during the next
few daze for two minutes at a time. Work out with
skill of a thousand mathematicians that this will
allow me SEVERAL DAZE worth of filming and
still leave 10 mins over for link shots of presenter
(moi) talking meaningfully about passing of time,
amassing of dog poo, convening of dossers Etck.
For first time am glad we live in lively area complete
with drug dealers, hookers Etck instead of sleepy
suburb where only street activity comes from soft
bounce of kiddies' pushchairs and only dog poo
from refined beumbes of poodles Etck.

Spend happy hour or so designing wooden steps
for Benjy so that he can sleepwalk over quicksand.

Feeling of unadulterated bliss somewhat muted
by thought of Only Mother possibly on verge of
committing adultery herself. Is it possible to
commit adultery if you are not married? Get V.
Worried and look up adultery in dictionary:
'Voluntary sexual intercourse of married person
other than with spouse.'

Phew. At least my Mother won't be an adulterer,
since she is (tragickly, in my view) not married to

**Rover considering whether Cats can commit adultery
(or whether adults can commit cattery)**

my Only Father. Unless Neville *is married. Would
that make her an adulterer? Worry, Worry.*

*Both parents mercifully at home this evening
and apparently talking (or at least grunting) to
each other. So decide to put off Worrying for a day
or two and revel in new-found happiness.*

*Have you noticed, Reader, that I have NOT
been Worrying what to wear for my date with
Adam? I am meeting him in one hour's time and I
have spent one hour fixing up video camera and
one hour on Benjy's swamp bridge . . . and this is
because, at last, I have found a boy who I don't
have to pretend to be someone else with. Adam,
after all, has seen me covered in purple dye and
cornflakes. He has seen me entwined with a bus
conductor, engulfed by falling cameras, stuffing my
fist in my mouth to stop myself laughing at Mogul
Mogul Junior the Third and blushing violently with*

the shame of Benjy's folder. He knows me. This must be the Real Thing.

Er, even so, I'll just spend the next 50 mins ironing my fog trousers, pressing my Hint-of-Ebony top, running a quick brush through my eyelashes Etck. And now I run to meet Him . . .

JEANS

Denim is V. Sexy on Right Person, but Naff when worn by leering teachers trying to look 'trendy' (a Kool werd from the 1970s that is now only Kool in the same sense as dead frog Etck).

And Jeans, when worn low on cat-size hips of Adam Stone, with tantalizing metal fly buttons Etck (whoops, family buke), remain, as they have done since first cowboy swung long limb from saddle and loped into Dead Crow salon, SEXiest item of

Builders' Bum Jeans Bulk Buy

fashion available in opinion of *moi*. V. Baggy grey ones revealing lots of beumbe Etck remain, as they have done since first builder shouted 'Oh wot a luvly pair' from scaffold, least SEXy item in fashion anals.

See also FASHION, TRAINERS.

JOBS

Gone are the daze, I am glad to say, when women were supposed to marry houses while men swanned about managing large companies and Doing It with their secretaries (also, digging mines, laying railroads, sewer pipes Etck and other unsavoury jobz we feminists wld like to write out of history, ahem).

But nowadaze both women and men have to slave away to make ends meet and unless they are DINKIES (Dual Income No Kids) they are probably paupers. Either you have several Jobz at once and no time for your family (who are therefore all on streets, hooligans, junkies Etck) or you have NO job and no money for your family (who are therefore all on streets, hooligans, junkies Etck).

Teenage Worriers keen to avoid being hooligans, on drugs, streets Etck or becoming parents of same need to develop LIFE-strategy-stuff NOW.

Do all the usual exam stuff which qualifies you to apply for Jobz Etck. When you have put off evil day for as long as you can, you have to apply for a Job. Ideally, you shld know how to spell (ho ho yeech).

JOB SEEKER'S TIP:
Write 6 letters for every vacancy using several aliases and all your relatives' addresses. This may give you a chance of an interview . . .

JOB FACTS:

In Little Britain, under-13s are not allowed Jobz
(even part-time ones) legally, so the only option is to
work casually for frendz, neighbours Etck. Obvious
stuff is car-washing, lawn-mowing, dog-walking. V.
Little skill needed (except for not getting windscreens
all smeary) but do not confuse and start mowing dog
or walking car (joy-riding seriously illegal). Some
people suggest baby-sitting, but if you are under 13
you shld still need a baby-sitter yourself and anyway
you are not yet the magical age to qualify as a True
Teenage Worrier.

Once you ARE a Teenage Worrier, you're allowed
to werk part time (not more than two hours on a
skule day) but you can't start before 7 a.m.

You're not allowed to do manual work (lifting
heavy stuff or working with dangerous machines)
until you're 16 and you can't work on the streets
(busking, selling stuff) until you're 18. As you can
see from under-age prostitutes, this law is badly
enforced.

Wages are usually rubbish for kids (even though
there is a measly minimum wage now, which is
better than olden daze when G. Chubb had to
scrub Lord Snooty's toilet for a handful of mouse
droppings) and if you kick up a fuss it is V.
Unlikely that you will keep Job as the employer
will get some other keen young person to exploit
instead. This is why El Chubb is so V. Keen on
Trade Unions, which at least gave the humble
werker a little bit of support.

If you're working for a parent these laws are flexible, which is why you often see tiny kids helping out in shops and getting V. Good at adding up.

Easiest job once you're about 15 is baby-sitting as long as you don't sit ON the baby, and do get the phone numbers of local doc, casualty, child's parents, grandparents Etck Etck. I even asked for the name of all the godparents when I baby-sat last month. Maybe that's why the parents got home so early, looking so Worried, and haven't asked me back.

See also CAREER, MONEY.

KAMA SUTRA

Indispensable Lurve Guide which shows you all the Lurve-making positions you can imagine (and quite a few you haven't thought of yet). How they do those positions is a mystery to *moi*, however. Are they made of elastic, or what?

KISSING (PART 3)

I have already dealt with this in my first two bukes. At length. But not long enough for my reader, it seems, as Teenage Worriers ask me 'How do you kiss?' Er . . . I haven't had enough practice. There was the incident where I cut my nose on Brian's specs. There was Pashione with Daniel that lasted three minutes. But did I do it well? He ran off with Aggy.

I should say that it affected parts of me I didn't know I had and evoked such thoughts as 'melting furnace and suffusing flames' Etck and it appeared to do the same for him. So obviously this kissing thing comes naturally at some point as long as you linger with it. But this LIFE buke is about getting Out in Werld and doing some other thingz so you're not gluming about thinking only of yr beLurved. I wish it werked for me.

LADS

Single blokes are V. Fashionable nowadays, viz: magazines like *Loaded*, *Pissed*, *Fart*, *Grunt* Etck and TV shows about men who try to Do It with anything even distantly resembling a gurl as long as it doesn't interfere with the taste of their TV dinners. Adam is a single bloke, of course, but he's as different from this kind of boy as if he had come from another planet, groan, glume, sigh Etck.

LANGUAGE

How you talk still has a V. Big effect on how you are perceived, according to surveys. 'RP' (received pronunciation or, in El Chubb's dictionary, Toffspeak) is yer basic BBC voice. If you speak like that, most British people (however they speak themselves) will think you are more intelligent, trustworthy Etck than if you drop yer aitches where they should be and add them where they hain't (as in calling an 'h' a 'haitch').

It sometimes seems that if you want to Get On, Rule Werld Etck you need either Accent or Attitude (preferably both). However, as L. Chubb, Karl Marx, Plato and other grate philosophers have often been heard to muse, LIFE is full of contradictions and lots of people rise to Top of heaving pile of yumanity without either Accent or Attitude (viz: Newspaper Bosses, Politicians Etck).

Brits are V. Bad at learning other people's languages, 'cos we are so snooty about our own lingo being the world's most popular, since the Americans speak it. Hence we expect everyone to learn it and if we go to France we do daft things like speak English in a French accent and hope they'll understand.

Loads of languages are becoming extinct: there are currently 2,500 languages in the world, but anthropologists reckon that in 23 years' time there may only be 60!! Where will the other 2,440 go to? Rescue a language by learning one today! And why not start with:

LETTIC
How cld I resist putting this in? It is the group of languages spoken by the old Prussians, the Lettish (mainly from Latvia) and Lithuanians. Let's learn it.

LIFE

Let me quote from the *Concise Oxford Dictionary*: 'State of functional activity and continual exchange peculiar to organized matter, and esp. to the portion of it constituting animal or plant before banana, animate existence, being alive . . .'

Yes, fellow Worriers! This is it! This is that great thingamajig we're experiencing. The Dict does not say 'banana', by the way, it uses that Other Werd about dying that rhymes with 'breath'.

But if LIFE only pertains to organized matter then what am I doing stuck in the middle of it? A tangled ball of wool is more organized than *moi* – and it is made of matter, surely. So which of us is the more alive?

As for functional activity – hmmmm. I s'pose I perform functions (many of them unmentionable in a family buke). But do I *have* a function? That is, a purpose in LIFE? And do I engage in continual exchange? Argggg.

This causes me to ponder on how little we can discover of the true yuman meaning of werds by simply looking them up in the dictionary.

EL CHUBB'S LIFE-TIPS:
*Now, you've already described what you LOOK like (see IMAGE section, above). But this is a much better exercise. Describe YOURSELF. Without *any reference to your looks at all*. Resist

'tall' or 'black' or 'skinny' or any of that stuff.
Think about what your family might like about
you. And your frendz. (If no family OR frendz, not
even one, then is there anything the social worker
might appreciate, or the goldfish?) Try describing
someone else in your LIFE this way:

'Very little conversation, but restful personality.
Never argues.' If I add 'Appears to enjoy swimming
in circles' you will see that I am describing a
goldfish. But the latter remark is based on a rather
low choice-threshold for a fish in a bowl . . . You
shld find it easier describing a dog or cat, and
easier still describing a person. Think *character*.

*GET OUT THERE! The best antidote to
Worrying about Yrself and how you look/seem/are
is to do something in the werld that helps you
forget. If you only hang out with other Worriers
examining yr spots, lanky wigs Etck (you must do
some of this, as you know by now) you are bound
to pine.

But if you go to films, clubs, get into team
sports, hobbies, music Etck Etck then the werld
opens up and you find you have something else to
Worry about (like whether you have perfect pitch,
can draw like da Vinci Etck), which is a whole lot
better than worrying about yr Image.

*ACCEPT YRSELF. There are bits you like,
bits you don't. Same is true of every person on the
planet. You're only a Yuman Bean, and there's only
so much a Yuman Bean can do (am I stringing you
along? Ha ha yeech).

*DON'T LISTEN TO HORRIBLE PEOPLE:
'Sticks and stones may break my bones but words
will never hurt me.'

There never was a more *un*-true rhyme in the
werld. But let's make it come true. Anyone who
says anything mean about the way you look (or the
way anyone else looks) just isn't worth bothering
about.

*ER, THINK POSITIVE: Ahem, as you know,
El Chubb is not always V. Good at this. Worrying
is not best route to Positive Thinking. But a handy
tip wld be to look at the descriptions you gave
above of the way you ARE. Then change any negative descriptions either to positive ones or to neu-
tral ones, eg (I'll take a *looks* example): 'I have a
vast, hideous nose' could become 'My hooter is like
a Roman Emperor's,' or 'On the Richter scale of
noses, mine would be high', or 'Thank God, I've
got a nose. What would I pick otherwise?' or 'I
love my nose! Without it, how would I smell?' (No
old jokes per-*lease*.)

By working this krafty Positive Thinking stuff, a
speechlessly shy person can become enigmatic, a
Crazed Worrier is transformed into conscientious
and caring, a bossy-boots becomes full of leader-
ship potential Etck Etck. NB: If you've only written
nice thingz about yourself in the first place you are
not a Worrier (tell me how you do it).

*DO GREAT WORKS: The Best People in
the werld did not do stuff because of what they
looked like but because of who they were.

They used talents to invent, change, campaign, make, build, paint, describe, analyse, dissect Etck Etck all the brilliant things on the planet. Only models and film stars rely on their looks. That is considerably less than 1% of the population, so why are we hung up on them? It is 'cos we think no one will Lurve us unless we're beautiful? But is that why we Lurve our frendz?

Teenage Worriers considering Grate Werks

LUXURY

Luxury is not just for the rich. Luxury is for You and Me, dearest Worriers. You do not need to sun yrself in foreign climes, bathe in champagne or ride wild white horses through the surf (nobody needs this, naturally, but a small amount of yearning is allowed): you can get DIY Luxury on tap at home, if only you organize yrself.

Luxury
Is two bags of fudge.

Luxury
Is Rover and a hot water bottle. Rover makes me sneeze, the HWB is leaky, but the moment of Luxury before the sneezing and the damp is worth it, oh Yes!

Luxury
Is curling up with Rover, fudge, hot water bottle, blanket, TV, Music, V.Good buke and being brought a cup of hot chocolate by my only mother. This happens when moon is blue, but I am even prepared to make my own Hot choccy in order to experience this remarkable glow.

Luxury

Is when the bath water runs hot (about twice a week in our house) and there is a half centimetre of Jumbo Bubblo left in Benjy's bubble bath.(My mother locks hers away, and benjy's, being V.Cheap, gives me eczema....but who cares?)For ten mins, until water is tepid. I can lie in scalding foam imagining I am Queen of Persia Etck.

Luxury

Is when there are three good programmes on the TV, it is pouring with rain outside and the heating's working (see bath, above).

Fudge de Luxe

CHAPTER EIGHT
MMMMMMZE TO
OOOOOOOZE

Oh, glorious Saturday morn . . .

I arrived on time, flushed yet serene. V. Worried to find that none of the films showing were called Large Door *and immediately experienced familiar sinking feeling as though lead weight were pulling me into Jurassic Swamp. Had I*

a) Gone to wrong cinema?
b) Been stood up?
c) Been victim of grisly hoax whereby a load of Adam's mates would jump out from behind a pillar jeering?

Oh me of little faith! There he was: a vision of flowing wig (gleaming midnight spirals . . .) and lissom limbs loping towards me, waving tickets for L'Âge d'Or *(French, of course). Don't ask me about the film. I was aware only of Adam's smouldering presence (of course it was a No Smoking cinema, you fuel) and the intense anticipation of the KISS. In fact, he was rather absorbed by the film and, er, did*

*not, sadly, do more than run his fingers shatteringly
through my wig Etck until later . . .*

*How is it possible to concentrate under such
circumstances? Nevertheless, I bluffed my way
interllekshually through the content of* L'Âge d'Or,
*amid the sweet nothings we exchanged afterwards,
over a stale chikko-burger and a flat Coke. We
talked of everything in the werld. My life has been
a pale shadow of an existence till now. We are
going to continue with the film course to get as
much as we can from it and to pursue our projects
despite Sleeve, then we will set up our own film
company:* Lettadam. *(The name may need some
fine tuning but is better, we thought, than*
Chubbstone.*) There are loads of places that will
give us dosh, he sez – organizations for Young Film
Makers Etck Etck and maybe we could even write
to Mogul. Yes! Adam believes in miracles! And so
do I! Together we can do it. Together.* Together . . .

*Now that I have been wined and dined (coked
and burgered sounds a trifle rude) by Adam Stone,
Wyoming-Grilled Chikko will never seem the
same . . . it is true what they say about Lurve –
it flourishes against the odds.*

*What cared we for the dog poo that we slid in?
What cared we for the abusive winos to whom we
scattered our few precious remaining coins? Or for
the litter that flapped against our thighs as we
ambled through the mean streets in the driving
rain, entwined in our mutual dream?*

When Adam laughed, the rain glistened on his

*sculpted brow just like in the movies and then, just
like in the movies, he clasped me to his manly chest
and . . . kissed me.*

Throb. Pulse. Meltdown.

*Alas, we cannot meet over the weekend as he
has to go to visit a sick aunt in Kent (had never
realized how many sick relatives there are in the
werld before), but I will see him on Thursday at
the course and we will make another date then!*

*My happiness knows no bounds. I yam a
woooman who has kissed ecstatically, Etck.*

*Today, I shall laze and dream and devote myself
to plans for* Lettadam . . . Chubbadam . . .
Lettystone . . . *in which our talents will mingle and
combine to surge forth and float to New Horizons
on wings of Art . . .*

ARG. You won't believe what has just happened.

*I was shuffling dreamily downstairs (having wal-
lowed in ecstatic memories of last night and re-read
above diary entry 6 times, wondering how better to
describe my rapture) when I glimpsed a letter on
the door mat. For moi.*

Letty, Letty, Letty!
My heart is breaking. I know you can never
forgive me, nor do I expect you to, but last night
I saw you kissing Adam Stone and I cannot bear
for you to be hurt again, my own, my dearest
sensitive flower!
Stone is two-timing you with that babe from LA.

I don't know if I should tell you this but when I saw you with another I knew what I should have known, long, long ago. That I love you, have always loved you. Dare I say it, WILL always love you!

Of course I expect nothing from you, except, perhaps, that you will allow me from time to time to take tea with you, just to be near you, and perhaps, one day, to take you to the theatre before you are married and whisked away from me for evermore.

All I do beg is that you find someone who will cherish you as I should have done and that you are not deceived by Adam Stone, who has broken hearts from here to Iceland (where his nature truly resides) and back.

If, by the smallest, tiniest, flimsiest, minutest chance, you wish to see me again, just to tell me you forgive me, I shall wait for you on Thursday after your Film Course. If you come out with Adam Stone, I shall know all is lost. If not, I'll see you by the bench round the corner (you remember the one – how could I forget!) where first we declared our love.

Forever yours,

Daniel.

Arggggggg. Adam Stone two timing me? Never!

But is that really an aunt he's visiting?

And what of Candice? Has she really gone back to LA or is she in fact in Kent?

The seeds of doubt are sown. Despair descends, gripping me in icy grip.

MANNERS

Manners used to be something you had to learn from etiquette bukes if you wanted to make it in a thing called 'Society'. For instance, a Real Lady would be someone who treats a duke and a dustman just the same. I wld certainly qualify as a Real Lady under this definition, if I knew any dukes. You can probably use a few rools even in today's don't-care-trample-on-a-pensioner-before-breakfast werld: Not farting and picking hooter in company, frinstance.

MODELS

See SUPERMODELS.

£ MONEY £ £ £ £ £ £

£ Q: *What is the worst way to spend a million pounds?*

(Think before you read the answer, as it is a V. Big insight of El Chubb's, and you won't get it unless you think. Have you thought? Go on, think again. I'll print the answer rather small so you don't see it until you've had a serious thought . . .)

A: Give 50p to two million people.

Arg. See? V. Worrying, espesh, for *moi* who is a socialist. But as you see, it is necessary to share, but wisely.

In order for us Teenage Worriers to enjoy the rest of our lives, we will need Money. But how much? Obviously if we're honest, a whole lot doesn't help that much, but it is better than none. What we NEED is to know we can have enough, and that is what the Govt over the last 15 years or so has tried to stop people hoping and believing. So everyone has been trying to make as much as possible in order to stash some away for rainy days, redundancies Etck Etck. El Chubb thinks the most Imp campaign of all is for real Social Security. Then people wld be happy to werk in decent caring professions like teaching, doctoring, social werk Etck and not feel failures 'cos they don't get free lunches, expense accounts Etck

Etck and not fear that they might be laid off anyway.

In the meantime there are some ways round having no dosh (which is the central state of the Teenage Worrier).

1) *Swap stuff*: Your frendz' bukes, CDs, clothes Etck may be boring to them and fascinating to you. You may even have something *they* want. Then swap it. You cld swap it for a month even, or for ever.

2) *Presents*: Instead of whingeing on about horrible things you've been given, how about making sure you get what you want at Christmas and birthdays? Ask for tokens or money, or for every Adult you know to band together for those astronomically expensive roller-blades Etck.

3) *Save*: In order to save, you got to have

Exploit the younger generation . . .

I'll swap you this LOVELY Noddy book for your brother's BORING old CD player....

something in the first place and in Hard Times like these there are Teenage Worriers who don't get anything at all. My Adored Father didn't even get a bus fare when he was a kid and had to walk 6 miles to skule as he never fails to remind *moi*. We all want a lot of stuff these days and we have to earn or save to get it rather than badger our poor old folks.

4) *Car Boot Sales*: Not bad for picking up bargains, prezzies Etck, also grate for getting rid of your parents' CDs Etck (just a joke). Snag is, you need a car, so co-operation from elder generation usually necessary.

5) *Get a Job*: There is a limit on what you are allowed to do until you're 18 (see JOBS) but here are

Unless you give impression of being able to clean and groom yrself, you may draw a blank . . .

a few tips until I get round to writing my major opus
(Latin for Grate Werk) entitled FIVE THOUSAND
WAYS TO EARN 50P:

*START A SERVICE: Instead of banging
hopelessly on doors only to be faced by disgruntled
residents complaining that you are ruining their
Sunday snooze, why not put cards through their
doors advertising yourself? i.e.: V. GOOD CAR-
WASHING/DOG-WALKING/PET-GROOMING/
WEEDING BY EXPERTS; BRILLIANT
DECORATING BY ZAK AND ZIP. Make *sure* a
sensible adult has checked out where you are going
to werk and that you *never* go into a strange house
alone!!!!! There's a lot of odd jobs you can do that
adults would prefer not to do and if you do them
really well you'll be asked back.

Also, you can swap a service for a service – ie:
offer to sweep up in the hairdresser's for a free hair-
cut, muck out riding stables for a free ride Etck.

*MAKE STUFF: You can sell hand-made cards
to local shops or any of your hobby-type stuff
(see HOBBIES) and even do a sign that goes with
them: HANDCRAFTED BY LOCAL TEENAGE
WORRIER, frinstance.

As any Worried Cynic knows by now, this is
unlikely to make your fortune. But it's worth
remembering that the V. Posh Department Store in
London, Horrids, started LIFE as a fruit & veg
stall in a market.

*HOLD AN AUCTION: Auctioning old clothes,
mother's furniture Etck is V. Good way of raising

BARGAIN EMPORIUM

Cheap'n'cheerful prezzies for the whole family for under a fiver each!

Roll of sticky Tape!
Barely used!!

"BALL-O-WOOL"

UNUSUAL SOCKS
Barely matching!
Seldom used!

Nearly new FORK.

FULLY POSEABLE DOGGY
Made of pipecleaners.

OLD COPIES of "Pony-4-U" News

BARGAIN! Fluff sculpture
Indispensable table
ornament.

Exquisite Bonsai twig.

ORIGINAL handpainting,
hand painted by El Chubb.

dosh, though L. Chubb's attempts to sell his own toys to her little brother Benjy have sadly failed: all the money he has is cardboard coins from his new Privatized Postperson Patricia Playset.

For other 4,997 ways to earn 50p send SAE to L. Chubb, kreator of Yuniverse. Do not expect reply, as I shall be cashing in the stamps. (This is actually good way to make Dosh – ie: put an ad in paper saying 'Make your fortune, enclose 50p plus SAE'. Then you write back telling person to put ad in paper Etck Etck. Prob illegal though, whinge.)

See also POCKET MONEY.

MUSIC

THE NICE GURLS (El chubb's dream band)

MUSIC

According to ye grate Bard Spokeshave, Music is s'posed to be the food of Lurve, sweet melodies flowing like crystal streams bearing Lurvers away to

a werld of perfect harmony Etck. On this evidence,
Spokeshave had clearly not visited the Toxic Rat
Klub in Werld's End Lane recently, because the
Music there makes you feel as if you've been
trapped inside a washing-machine.

Let me say, dear student of LettyLIFE, I am a big
fan of all kinds of Music, because I do think that it
reaches the parts other creative stuff doesn't reach,
including admittedly some parts (ahem, wince,
tingle, twitch) that the Guardians of Our Souls are
always flapping about when they moan that all
Pop Music other than Cliff Richard represents
Catastrophic Moral Decline Etck (and if they only
like Cliff Richard then they could be in favour of
Catastrophic Mental Decline anyway). Music is
about the Whole Person, it seems to *moi*, body and
mind together, and that's why it has such a big effect
on us, and espesh on Teenage Worriers whose bodies
and minds are entwined in such an intense way,
chance would be a fine thing, moan, whinge Etck.

There are many musical tastes in the Chubb
household. Adored Mother thinks Mozart is like
the quality of light summer, Beethoven like the
fearful restlessness of the elements, the Bee Gees
like the kind of men she wished Adored Father
had been, nice arty white suits and long hair,
Sensitive Feelings, voices like choirboys Etck.
She recently asked me if Underground, Garage,
Jungle, or House were new forms of Teenage
Habitat . . . Adored Father has big collection of
Heavy Metal records, but when pressed admits he

MIAOOOOOOOOOorrr
MeeEAaaaaaooou
Meeeaouiweeeou
Prmffrk

Rover's love song . . .

can't remember any of the songs, due to chemically induced confusion when originally experiencing same. Benjy likes banging a tin tray on the side of his head whilst attempting to play 'Frère Jacques' on the recorder one-handed.

For *moi*self, I like old Art Skule rock (Sonic

Beaver Etck) because it sounds like bedraggled, intense types trying to make sense of an alien world (like *moi*), some dance music, old Brit classical composers like Elgar and Vaughan Williams who makes me cry and want to be a horse, and some of Ashley's jazz records, even if they do sound a bit like people doing algebra out loud. Music is the food of LIFE, sez *moi*, and if things go on the way they are it might be the closest to pashione I'm going to get, sniff, whinge, cower, suck thumb for want of better things (a message from the Moral Decline of the Nation Dept), mope, kick Etck Etck.

Learning a Musical Instrument, however, is one of LIFE's grate Joyz, I have observed from those of my frendz lucky enough to have

a) Thought of it themselves
b) Been made to do it by their parents
c) Had enough dosh for lessons.

Teenage Worriers in Sluggs orchestra always seem somewhat Less Worried than the rest of us. Playing Music seems to have given Meaning to their LIFE.

Surveys now seem to suggest that learning about Music early is good for all other kinds of learning (also good for soul Etck). But the Govt doesn't seem V. Interested and there are hardly any proper music teachers in Primary Skules.

I didn't even get to play recorder, though I am

glad to (or sad to) say Benjy now has opp of learning this for free and I think I can stand the noise as long as it keeps him from Worrying about floors for a few more moments. I wish I had learned

1) Piano
2) Cello
3) Saxophone
4) Double Bass.

But I have finally gathered up ye courage to ask
Sluggs Music Dept if I can learn Accordion!!
My reasons are: no one else at skule plays it, so I
can't be compared to anyone; and also, the piano
teacher told me she has one and wld Lurve to teach
someone. Hold your breath for Letty Chubb, great
Accordionist. I can see self now, in French beret
Etck.

See also CLUBS.

The accordion is sad and
happy at once, like *moi*

NAMES

Those of us struggling under burdens like Scarlett
(a result of my selfish Mother's obsession with
Gone with the Wind) need solace when it comes to
the name business. I am hoping to get Adam to call

me Diana, as in proud, goddess-like creature, and our offspring will be David and Daisy, enabling us to live in 4D (four dimensions, so there) without having to time travel.

NAPALM

Q: Should you drop a jellied petrol bomb made from thickening agent, naphthalene and coconut oil on to babies when you know that it will burn their skin off?
A: Not really, but we did.
   Well, the Americans did in the Vietnam War.
   I put this in because it's clear that individual

American Teenage Worriers (the average age of the soldiers who fought the war was 19) would have answered 'No' to the above question. But they did it anyway, as a group, and under orders.

EL CHUBB's LIFE-TIP: Question orders. Question causes. Question Big Ideas. You could seem to be the lone voice against dictatorship. But where there's one voice, others will follow.

NATURAL

The use of this werd in ads for cosmetics Etck has always amused Yrs Truely vastly. You can spend a LIFEtime achieving that Nachural look. I am still offering El Chubb's Vampire (I mean Vamp) make-up kit to anyone who sends me a cosmetic ad without the word Nachural in it.

However, being Nachural in LIFE shld mean being yourself, which has to be a pretty Good Thing to be. I have tried V. Hard to be someone else for large chunks of my short-ish existence but I always end up being me in the end and wonder why I bothered. We're not talking about the way you LOOK here, although leaving yourself pretty much as you are seems V. Reasonable to *moi*, but the way you act and feel and talk and move.

People are always trying to improve themselves. But who for? Their parents? Their bosses? Their

Butch is brilliant
at ballet

Rosalie rollerblades
to Rachmaninov

L. Chubb Motto (No. 2468):

Harriet hugs hedgehogs

Cuthbert collects cat cards

Rover reminisces about rat ratatouille

BE YOURSELF

Teachers? Some Lurve-Object? OR an Almighty Being who is looking down from on high and saying, 'You SLOUCH. Stand UP!'

Or 'Have you seen the state of your wig/hairbrush/room?'

Or 'We Godz hate freckles and you won't get into heaven wearing an anorak.'

Going for what YOU find interesting is the key to a good LIFE and to know what that is, you need to know who you ARE. So knowing your Nachural Self is a V. Good thing to start with.

Here are some ways:

1) Think about what you LIKE. Not what is fashionable. You might really like Elgar's Cello Concerto better than Bean and the Maggots (currently Number One, in case you didn't know) but be too ashamed to admit it, even to YOURSELF. See how daft that is?

2) Wear the colours you like. Yes! Even beige! (Just don't expect me to talk to you.)

3) If you like reading *Thrills & Swoon* you are allowed. Just 'cos I can't get past the first page of those bukes without throwing up, it doesn't matter.

4) If you want to dance all night and snort Coke . . . don't. knowing who you are means knowing how to take care of who you are. Doing illegal stuff is not taking care of yourself. Hurting other people's feelings isn't either.

If you pretend to be different in order to catch a

Lurver or make a frend, then they'll find you out
sooner or later or else you'll be pretending all your
LIFE.

RULES OF DECORUM FORBID:
- Total lack of washing.
- Farting, nose-picking Etck in company (though
see nose-picking for campaign against this
foolish prejudice).
- Saying exactly what you think, when you
think it. Think it, but don't always say it. It
could hurt someone else.
- Physical or mental violence.
- Public nudity. (Don't really understand this
rule, either, though it wouldn't suit *moi* as I
need four layers at least until June, then back
on again in Sept.)

<u>Avoid</u> <u>Nudity</u> <u>with</u> <u>El Chubb</u>

Bobble hat (in
salmon &
turquoise)
knitted by
Granny Chubb

Scarf (in
Mustard
Lime &
Maroon)
ditto

NEIGHBOURS

V.V.V. Imp to like your neighbours if at all poss and also to avoid watching the TV programme of the same name as scientists employed by L. Chubb have revealed brain damage resulting from prolonged exposure to same.

REASONS TO LIKE NEIGHBOURS

* They will have spare set of keys for those many occasions on which you have lost yours.
* They will let you sit by their radiator when you have ice inside your windows.
* They will give you thimbleful of milk, sugar Etck which your Mother is so V. Bad at remembering to buy.
* They MAY even let you use their phone (as long as you have appropriate dosh) when yours is cut off because your irresponsible, uncaring Adults have not paid bill.

They can, in short, be frendz against cruel werld.

So if you hate their kidz who go to the Nobs Academy, or have horrible haircuts, then stifle it. If their window box falls on your foot, see a doc but don't sue. Neighbourhoods are dwindling. If you've got one, treasure it.

NITS

You know what these are. Call them pendiculosis, if you prefer. If you've never had them, tell me your secret, as London Skules are their favourite nesting place (or rather the wigs of the unfortunate inhabitants). Some people still think it is a sign of dirtiness to have nits. Not so. They don't care if your hair is dirty Or squeaky clean; they simply jump skittishly from wig to wig in a completely indiscriminate manner and do not know if you're a Nice Person or not.

The only sensible way to get rid of these little blighters is to comb hair regularly with a fine-tooth comb. Lotions and potions contain chemicals and have to be used on a rotational basis anyway as the Super-nits of today have become resistant to them.

METHOD: Wash wig; dollop on loads of conditioner; comb carefully with V. fine-tooth comb (you can get them from chemist; metal ones are best) over a bit of kitchen roll. If any Nits emerge, then repeat process every three days for a couple of weeks. And enjoy a Nit-free LIFE (or at least a few Nit-free weeks). Arg.

NOSE-PICKING

Underrated pleasure thought repellent by those who haven't discovered its joys and hidden by those who have. This is the last guilty refuge of the Teenage Worrier but begs the question of manners, morals Etck. Frinstance, how many people have you seen mown down, slaughtered, decimated, tortured, violated Etck Etck on TV and in movies? And how many have you seen picking their noses?

Ask yourself: is this a true, fair, or sane picture of the Yuman Condition?

If you wish to complain about a lack of nose-picking on TV write to TV bosses.

NUCLEAR POWER/ENERGY

V. Big Worry for all Yoof as this source of energy still
dominates our lives and one small mistake can result
in a Chernobyl (the Russian nuclear station that hit
meltdown and killed a lot of people and wrecked the
surroundings). Current ways of getting rid of nuclear
waste seem unsatisfactory. This is an understatement.

To campaign for Safe Energy, join an
environmental group.

NUN

What I will become if LIFE goes wrong. Sigh.

OLD AGE

In my exhaustive surveys about what Teenage
Worriers Worry most about, I found that pensions
(surprise, surprise) come V. Low on the list. But it
is my job to edukate, instrukt Etck. So here is a
little lecture:

1) Old People sometimes sound like Boring Old
Twits who go on about the same things over and

over, forget they told you the thing they're telling you five minutes ago, complain about Yr Manners/Hair/Clothes/Language/Music Etck Etck. Sometimes they do this because they really are Old Twits, but those are prob also the people who were Young Twits first and just haven't changed much. The others are qu. likely doing it because most of the people they know, including their own off-spring and the Teenage Worriers that have ishooed therefrom, don't bother to listen to them, so they just keep repeating it in the hope that eventually someone will hear, like shipwrecked sailors throwing lots of bottles with notes in into the ocean.

2) Old People need decent pensions. They were young once. You will be old one day. They fought wars, werked hard, blah blah to look after offspring, defend democracy Etck, and are now on scrap heap of poverty. Worry about them now and it will make V. Big Diff to whether or not you are condemned to become an Old Age Worrier yrself.

OMELETTE

If you learn nothing else from this humble tome, you can at least learn simple cooking. Then you can convince parent this is worthwhile buke.

Put a very little (VERY little – very very little) butter in non-stick pan. Get it V. Hot. Break two

eggz into mixing bowl. Stir them up and add a
pinch of salt. Pour eggz into pan so they look nice
and flat like pancake. Get fish slice and *as soon as*
edge of egg looks stiffish, lift it up, tilt pan so that
runny egg goes under stiff bit. Continue until it's
JUST not runny. If you go on any more, it gets like
plasterboard. Take omelette out of pan. Eat. If
desired, start off by browning chopped onions,
bacon, peppers, ham, other goodies and by grating
cheese into eggz. Add eggz to other stuff and cook
as above.

Most Teenage Worriers don't know how to make
an omelette. That's because our lousy parents just
take a fish finger out of the ice compartment and
stick it in a pan. If only they taught us gourmet
cooking *à la Chubb* we wld be much healthier.

OMENS

XYZ Files, Paranormal stuff Etck has been all the rage for a while on TV but they are qu. bad for superstitious Teenage Worriers in the humble opinion of L. Chubb. We have enough to Worry about, wot with black cats, ladders, months with '13' in them Etck Etck. I prefer not to lie awake wondering if Zolga the Nerd is about to materialize in my bedroom and whisk me off for SEX-experiments Etck.

Whooooooooo ooOO
↖ wind
Blinding flash ✴
↖ Lightning, or electricity
on blink

SCREECH
↖ you have trodden on
cat's tail

Horrible squeaks
↖ did you oil your
bike?

El Chubb's pocket guide to Things-that-go-Bump-in-the-Night.

CHAPTER NINE
PPPPPPEEEEEEZE

But wait, what light through yonder winder gleams?
Adam Stone has betrayed me, woe and glume

BUT

Daniel Hope loves me still.
Can it be true? I am awash with emotion as the
iceberg of my heart softens, melts, cascades into a
flood of longing . . .
I had turned my back on him, knowing he would
never Be Mine. How faithless I have been, to think
of Another when obviously Daniel's relationship
with Sara Spiggott was profoundly superficial and
he was yearning for me all along.
At long last, he has seen the error of his ways
and realized where his true Lurve lies.
Adam Stone already seems just a blip in the
steady graph of my eternal Lurve for D. Hope,
now honed on the furnace of adversity Etck Etck.
There is no doubt in my heart. I shall fly to the
bench immediatement *(well, on Thursday after*
class anyway) and swear unswerving devotion
to Daniel.

Meanwhile I shall enjoy going on film course tomorrow and ignoring Adam Stone. Heh! Heh! Mad cackle of triumph Etck.

Must admit to Worry over Father, whose glume deepens as each day passes with no news of his buke. Has it really sunk without trace? Is fiction as fickle as fact? Is the world of bukes as unpredictable as the werld of Un-true Lurve?

If only my Adored Father had turned his talents to the micro-chipo like boring Neville then we could be champagne socialists and my Mother wld never look at Another. Glume, despond.

THURSDAY:
V. Interesting film course today. Sleeve has finally woken up to my talent, rolled himself up Etck and has paid teensy fee of £5 to option my pix of Aggy and siblings for further use. Meanwhile I am developing film storyboard re Granny Chubb, which he says is 'V. Promising'. Preen Etck. (Wait till he sees my video of a London street overflowing with crime, grime, corruption Etck.) Moiself overflowing with new-found confidence re Daniel. I barely noticed Adam Stone except to think he looked somewhat on the lanky side and that his hair was more greasy than shiny. I contrived to step on his foot, however, as I left.

He ran down the stairs after me and grabbed me roughly by the arm. How dare he? I shrugged him off. (Have read about people shrugging Despised

Ones off in bukes, and it is easier than you think, even with shoulders like mine.)

'What's up?' he queried with startling originality.

'Nothing whatsoever,' I swiftly replied with rapier-like wit, sarcasm Etck. 'Hope you had a ovely time in Kent.' And added as a parting shot, 'With Candice.'

Fled into night, pausing only to notice a look of bewilderment on Adam's face – the face I once thought dear. But where his image was, now shines only Daniel . . . who even now I fly to meet . . .

Furry hot water bottle. Essential pajama accessory

PAJAMAS

Have just discovered you can spell pyjamas this way too. What to wear to bed is a Big Worry for *moi*, as I hate those dinky nightie thingz with pink teddies or bows on but I can't qu. bring myself to wear the boyz stuff either, which is usually covered in supper heroes or American baseball logos. I need a nice stripy nightshift made of V. Warm stuff. Or plain red pyjamas. If you have a pair, cld you write in and tell me where you got them? Meanwhile, I recommend my current suave style of four of Only Father's old T-shirts and a jumper.

PANDORA

Famous character of Greek myth. She was a
Naughty Gurl who opened a box she wasn't
supposed to open. Out flew every horrible thing in
the werld: Pestilence, Famine, Plague, Glume, Dume
Etck Etck. So these things weren't here before?
Come on. Pull the other one. But a 'Pandora's Box'
has come to mean something you shouldn't delve
into . . . and there are such things, of course, like
secrets that someone else is guarding. One good
thing about the Pandora story is that she didn't
move fast enough to get the lid back on in time to
stop the last little thing fluttering out of the box.
That little thing was HOPE. And it flutters round
still, guarding us from despair for eternity.

PARENTS

*NB True, even if you've
never met them*

You can't help having Parents, though they cld
have helped having you, which is the source of a
famous cry of the desperate Teenage Worrier, 'I
never asked you to have me in the first place.' One
of the massive Probs of LIFE that has to be faced is
that Teenage Worriers have at some time in our
Teenage Worrying years to stand up to our Parents
and Become Ourselves, and Adored Parents have to
realize this has got to happen, and not fight against

You better believe it

Parents, part 2864

it. Sometimes, of course, we may be headed on V. Self-Destructive course that Lurving Parents are morally obliged to try to guide us away from, but some time between their own Wild Yoof of Doing It, Abusing Bod With Dodgy Thingz Etck and becoming Responsible Citizens many Parents unfortunately lose the ability to distinguish between the normal Luny Behaviour of The Young, and the conviction that their beLurved Ickle Babas have fallen into the hands of Drug Fiends, Slave-Traders, Group SEX Cults Etck. This can affect the judgement of Parents: we have to Deal With this, and whether we have to Deal With It kindly or unkindly can be to do with how bad their judgement has become.

But I also have a Thought of Chairman Chubb: most Parents, except for V. Crazed Ones, want nothing more from their children than that they should be Happy. Their idea of Happiness may be different from ours sometimes, but that doesn't matter. They also have to deal with V. Diff psychological thingz like seeing us grow into clever, desirable (chance wld be a fine thing, sniff, grump, moan), energetic beingz with good memories Etck, who don't get puffed running upstairs, just at the time of LIFE when they're having trouble with all these thingz themselves. Bear this in mind before calling Adored Parents Uncaring, Hateful, Interfering Stupid Scumbags, O Fellow Teenage Worriers. It will all happen to us one day. NB: If I could only follow own rools, wot a haven of sweetness and light our little hovel wld become . . .

PARTIES

Although Tragick LIFE-Worries like whether I'll be mistaken for a twiglet prevent *moi* from attending more than one party every decade or so I believe it is V. Imp for Teenage Worriers to celebrate LIFE at all opportunities. It helps events to stand out from the usual Mists of Glume, and gives you Memories to Treasure Etck. The rich tapestry Etck is throbbing with Special Moments if only we can seek them out. NB: Celebration Parties can be V. cheap and the best thing is, YOU are in control. Viz: Get everyone to bring pack of crisps and V. Unhealthy drink. All you have to do is provide hovel.

EL CHUBBO'S LIST OF THINGS TO CELEBRATE
   1) Day you learnt to walk (probably, like me, you have no idea which day this was, but *some* people's adoring parents keep baby bukes with these cutesy details in and you may as well make some use of them that isn't nauseatingly embarrassing). Ditto first smile, tooth Etck. If not blessed with Lurving family who bothered to write such thingz down (MY family certainly didn't), then celebrate fact you ever learnt to walk at all! Think how V. Hard this was to do. You only have to watch toddling infants tripping over bits of fluff, crashing to floor, wailing piteously, hauling selves up only to soldier on and hurtle to floor again to see what incredible determination this task takes. If only we

cld apply such effort to all the tasks of LIFE the werld wld be a Better Place. As for learning to talk! It takes just three years! How come Sluggs Comprehensive can't teach us French then?

2) Your first period! Radical! (I know some of you are still waiting – I waited long enough, and if you are a boy you shld be prepared to wait as long as possible, ie: Ever. How about a voice-breaking party for you? Squeeeeak, grunt.)

3) If you add on ALL your family's weddings, b'days, new jobs, redundancies Etck you cld have a

party every week of the year. Think of how it will be in 30 years' time when your own simpering offspring ask: 'Where did 'ooo an' dada meet?' And you reply: 'At the birthday party for my best frend'z tortoise's daughter.'

PARTY-WORRIER'S TIPS:
* Go with frend if poss. This helps you get in the door without fainting and may give you someone to talk to (until frend is whisked away by wunderbabe into snogging corner leaving you glumier than before).
* Wear something V.V. Simple, pref in shade of Ebony or Fog. Christmas tree balls on ears OK for Christmas. Also V. Comfy for quick getaway. No glass slippers.
* Eat before you go. This will soak up any stray alcohol you may mistakenly imbibe (ahem) and will compensate for V. Unpleasant snacks to be found at most parties, ie: cheesy wotnots mixed with fag ash, 'French' bread with consistency of iron bar Etck.
* Remove food from face, teeth Etck before entering party venue, unless you want to be

← Kool 'Hint of Midnight' Designer Top.

← kool 'Touch of Cave' Joggers.

Moi: enjoying a party

229

that person with the special peanut butter and spinach smile.

Arg. How is humble *moi* to give this kind of advice when I always end up hiding in loo, under pile of coats Etck? Go to cinema instead.

PERIOD

Your Periods will start sometime between the ages of 10 and 17. if you haven't started at 16 and are also exhibiting no other signs of puberty (eg: body hair, bazooms), get a doctor to check it out.

Irregular Periods are V.V. Common, particularly early on in yr cycle, so don't fret if you have a Period and then don't have one for several months. It takes a while for them to get going. Once Periods have really got started, they go on. And on. Dum-di-dum. Roughly every 28 days. Tra-la-la. Whatever you do. Dum-di-dum. This is a Fact of LIFE and shld not be regarded as a matter of glume, dume Etck as most Teenage Worriers will not get particularly bad cramps or particularly bad PMT (Pre Menstrual Tension). Those who do, however, shld retire with vast hot water bottles and weep for three days. There are still mothers who think their daughters shouldn't swim, have nookie Etck while they have a Period. There may be

V. Good reasons for abstaining from activities –
eg: sloth, disinclination – but, unless you are one
of unlucky few with V.V. Bad Periods, menstrua-
tion is not one of them. And, as a Proudly-Slothful
Worrier, I hate to admit it, but exercise is sometimes
the best thing for cramps, as it increases blood
flow and stops clots and therefore stops cramps
(which is your trusty bod trying to expel clots).
Hey-ho. One note of glume, however. If you *do*
have V.V. bad pains, it could be worth seeing yr

doc, just in case it *is* a sign of something wrong (like endometriosis). Aargh! Worry, worry.

You can, in fact, do anything you like when you have a period but you also must wear towels or tampons. Some Teenage Worriers are scared of tampons 'cos they think they might disappear up inside. Not possible. The vaginal passage is completely closed by the neck of the womb (cervix), so once you've put a tampon in, it can only come out one way. However, it IS possible to forget tampons are there and this can lead to infection or even Toxic Shock, which is V. Dangerous. It's better to use the new whizzo shaped towels (despite nauseating ad for wings Etck) when you can. Never use tampons that are more absorbent than you need for your flow (do NOT be that gurl who bungs in a super-plus in case she comes on) and don't leave them in overnight. You can always use pads then.

El Chubb's Campaign for Embarrassment-Free Periods is gaining support. A large sculpture made of pads, towels, tampons through the ages is to be erected in Sluggs playground next term. The teachers don't know this, but the gurlz are plotting. Heh! Heh!

PESSIMIST

A pessimist always sees the down side. If an optimist

says the cup is half full, the pessimist will say it's half empty (reverse, if liquid is deadly toxin). I am V. Worried that Worriers are essentially pessimists, as they are always thinking: 'What if?' ie: it is a perfectly nice day full of sunshine, cheer, little birdies humming in breeze Etck and everyone will

be skipping happily about in flimsy garb and
Worrier will say what if Hurricane Xerox emerges
from nowhere bringing Devastation in its wake?

LIFE-TIP: If you feel you have a tendency to
look on down-side, remember El Chubb's two fave
sayings:

'LIFE is just a bowl of Cherry stones' and

'When one door closes, another door closes.'

If you can do better than this, award yrself small
LIFE-enhancing treat – ie: a single Smartie Etck.

PETS

Are a V. Big solace in times of glume. Even a
goldfish is better than no pet, though watching
washing go round in machine is nearly as fun.

See CATS, DOGS, GERBILS, HORSES.

PHILOSOPHY

Philosophy is what you don't usually get to study
until 'A' level, which is a V. Big shame since it is
really the study of thought and how to think and
therefore one of the keys to the key to the key
(if there is one) to all of Yuman LIFE. It includes
seeking after wisdom generally in order to

My Dream Pet (don't tell Rover)

understand the Nachur of the Yuniverse (at which physics excels) and to werk out a moral philosophy (known as Ethics). Which is what we all need all the help we can get in doing.

'Philosophy' comes from Greek, and means 'a love of wisdom'. I Have a Dream, that one day I will have a colossal buke-lined study full of the Great Thoughts of V. Clever People, like they advertise in those brochures for encyclopaedias Etck, with everything in red leather with gold lettering Etck to make it look V. Old and Trustworthy. Then I wld travel with my BeLurved on a Great Philosophical Journey interrupted by bouts of Doing It and Making V. Brilliant Films, until I was the Wisest Person on Earth and people wld come to me for Guidance.

Philosophical Stuff includes Metaphysics (nachur and future of The Yuniverse), Idealism (whether the Werld is only Thought, and inside our heads), Materialism (whether the Werld is only Stuff – 'Matter' – outside our heads), Dualism (Thought and Stuff mixed together), Logic (how we werk things out), Ethics (Doing The Right Thing), Aesthetics (how we decide what's Byootiful Etck) and so on.

You can see from this brief Dirty Thumbnail sketch that Philosophy is a lot different to playing DOLPHS, CITYSCAPE Etck, and a pretty heavy business. Different countries also go in for different kinds of Philosophies, like the ones influenced by Buddhism in the East, by Materialism in Europe

(Marxism Etck), by Science, by Art, and lately by
Komputer Science. A new Philosophy brought
about by Komputers is called Chaos Theory, which
sounds like the closest Philosophy has so far got to
the LIFE of El Chubb and her Adored Family. If
you want to get into Philosophy, you need to study
it at skule if you can, and then at college or university, because it isn't something you can get together
by reading half a buke and calling it a day.

PHOBIAS

Phobias are being scared of something for no good
reason. At least, that's what the eggsperts say, but
I'm scared of thingz quite a lot of the time and the
reasons always seem perfectly good to me – it's
reasonable to be scared my Adored Parents will
have us all Repossessed frinstance, the way they
stumble aimlessly through LIFE; reasonable to be
scared I might wake up one morning to find myself
turned into a giant pluke; reasonable to be scared
God might not be Out There and the Werld is just
a Virtual Reality game run by anoraked aliens from
Ursa Minor Entertainments Corp.

Well, of course, it's not reasonable reeeely, because
the odds on encountering these thingz statistically are
about the size of my bra measurements. But there are
zillions of types of Phobias, including fear of enclosed

Benjy has attack of Floor Phobia

spaces (claustrophobia), open spaces (agoraphobia),
water (hydrophobia), animals (zoophobia) and floors
(Benjyphobia), and it's a good idea to try to deal with
them if you're afflicted by same, because otherwise
it's like trying to run through LIFE as if it were a
three-legged race, with this great mad, cackling,
nagging, finger-wagging THING tied to your leg. And
if they really get in the way of enjoying yrself, then
you could need professional help like psychotherapy.
DO see your doc if this is the case.

I have many minor obsessional habitz (fringe-
twisting, touching things twice, fear of odd
numbers Etck) but have just discovered brand-new
one to add to long list of obsessional disorders
Etck suffered by Chubb Family: Acrophobia. This is

A touch of Acrophobia on high kerb stones can make even short journeys problematic

related to Abseiling – an abnormal dread of heights. What is abnormal about this, for goodness' sake? I recall with horror becoming very dizzy crawling out onto a window-ledge to rescue an escaped Benjy when he was entrusted to the tender care of Yrs Truely, and had it not been for Said Sibling showing maturity beyond his years in turning around and V. Sweetly calming *moi* down until we could climb inside again, I don't know what would have happened. If we hadn't been on the ground floor I might have had a V. Serious Panic Attack.

PICNIC

One of El Chubb's favourite pastimes is going for
Picnics. *What?!* I hear you cry? You, who like best
to curl up with Rover, fudge, hot water bottle Etck?
Yes. *Moi*. I like to check out that Hurricane Xerox is
not lurking behind the sun, which means I will
watch the weather forecasts closely for many daze
before embarking on a Picnic adventure. But I like it
reminding me of my Yoof. I like packed lunches. V.
Crusty bread with loads of butter, cheese, jam,
strawberries, fudge Etck and a big flask of cherry
fizz. You then get to do absolutely nothing for four
hours except eat grub and gaze at little fluffy clouds,
dangle feet in tinkling stream, muse on wonders of
Mother Nachur Etck. Our local park, dog poo to
the left, rubbish dump to the right, is not the ideal
venue for this idyll – although I have been known to
sneak off here with Benjy and a couple of Teddies to
relive childhood. He likes to take a V. small packed
lunch for each Teddy, consisting of one Smartie, a
cherry tomato and a honey sandwich. A-ah BLESS.
But country-dwelling Teenage Worriers shld find
ample opps for this most cheap of pursuits.

PIERCING

Piercing noses, ears Etck used to be V. Naughty but

now most of Benjy's frendz' mums have rings through their tongues Etck it is looking a bit old-fashioned to *moi*. Anyway, I don't even fancy pierced ears *moi*self, and am always looking for nice clip-on hoops to decorate my shell-like lobes (cross between those of Dumbo's relative and the Mad Hatter).

PIZZA

The fast food of the 80s is here to stay. Akshully, Pizzerias go back a lot further than you might think: the first Pizzeria opened in America in 1895, and the boom in Pizza bars and restaurants really got going after WW2, when American servicemen returning from Italy created a demand for what was originally a Sicilian dish. However, it seems to me that in the age of Virtual Reality (see VIRTUAL REALITY) Etck the present method of Pizza deliveries on the back of mopeds driven by young escaped lunies with Visual Challenges is out of date and that it can only be a matter of time before a Fax-A-Pizza service is with us.

N.B. Lots of painting of Fruit Etck. But V. few portraits of pizza, I note.

PLAY

You may think, now you are a Teenage Worrier,

that you are supposed to stop Playing. Most Adults, when they were about our age, thought the same thing, which is why they turned into the panic-stricken nervous wrecks who now rool our lives. But the secret is to go on Playing for the rest of yr LIFE. How to play

a) Cheaply and
b) Legally

is the main prob, as Adventure Playgrounds Etck are beginning to lose their appeal (although a simple swing still feels grate to El Chubb – am I retarded? Worry, worry).

It is no coincidence that musicians *Play* music, or that actors put on *Plays*, or that professional sport people *Play* sport . . . Playing is about having a good time and if you can find werk that is fun, then you will never have to stop Playing for the rest of your LIFE. You can see who really enjoys their werk in the Adult Werld – musicians, obsessive scientists, inventors, footballers, actors Etck.

L. Chubb's LIFE-TIP: Have FUN.

POCKET MONEY

This is like wages-for-kids. It should be yours to spend exactly as you like and it shouldn't be

Q: What do all these people have in common?

A: Zero dosh

stopped, really, 'cos you can't get sacked by your parents and the only way their wages are stopped is if they get fired. But . . . whatever your folks give you, big or small, it is never enough. It is, though, probably all they can afford (unless they are V.V. Rich – and if they are, then they aren't being mean, just trying to let you discover meaning of money Etck Etck, blah drone). Teenagers, like pensioners, come in all shapes, sizes, colours and characters. But what they have in common is that they are Poor.

See also, JOBS, MONEY.

POETRY

One of LIFE's great solaces, Poetry can comfort Teenage Worriers in times of glume and dume and it is V. Imp to write a lot of it at our age. In fact, if you have got to 17 without writing a poem, it may be worth sitting down and having a go.

An essential LIFE-Item in El Chubb's artillery for fending off dume is a personal Limerick. It can be done even if you have V. Difficult name like my own. Viz:

There was a young woman called Scarlett
Who objected to rhyming with harlot
'Don't call me a whore,'
She declared with a roar
'Or I'll soon give you something to snarl at.'

NB: This will work equally well with Charlotte. If you are called Betty you can nick my other one:

> *There was a young person named Letty*
> *Who said of a bloke she had met, 'He*
> *Would be perfectly nice*
> *If ploughing through ice*
> *For he puts me in mind of a Yeti.'*

I'm qu. proud of the double rhyme in the second line and am wondering if a career as a lyricist beckons (phew, blush). I had been working on one for Adam but was having trouble with ('Macadam'? 'Madam'? Etck). And what about Daniel? ('Spaniel'?). Answers on a postcard please.

POLITICS

Harry Stotle (not really! *Aristotle*, you lunes), the famous Greek thinker and Person, said that 'Man is a Political Animal', and I think he must have meant Gurlz too. What was he on about? The dictionary says Politics is about governing, and when we were all stumbling around in woad clubbing each other Etck, there prob wasn't a lot of governing going on, but maybe that's why Harry Stotle thought the Idea caught on in the first place. As Yuman Groups got larger, they had to werk out how to organize

But NOW New Labour has more gurlz. V. Good. And, El Chubb pleased to note, not ALL of them V. worried about LOOKS.

themselves, agree on Leaders, establish laws Etck, so they didn't have to go round clubbing each other at random all the time but could work out who were the Right People to Club and who weren't, which is pretty much how Politics werks today.

Most Teenage Worriers are V. Political, which means they hate politicians but care V. Much about the things that politicians ought to be caring about. It is Teenage Worriers who do V. Brave actions like tunnelling under motorways to try to Save Trees Etck. We know that writing to MPs will never

A little pun – Polly tics

achieve so much as Direct Action and we also know that MPs who complain about their salaries Etck are Out-of-Touch with most folk who are

a) Earning less
b) Earning nothing.

But in my better moments I can't help thinking that Politics would be a V. Good Thing to go into if you think you're a strong enough person to keep Yr Principles against all the pressures you come up against. If this is yr LIFE-choice, Good Luck.

NB: Campaign for the new Teenage Worriers' Party (see PARTIES ho ho).

PROMISCUITY

Means sleeping around, which has always been V. Acceptable for Boyz but not for Gurlz. AIDS has given everyone a new reason not to do this (although there are still V. few Teenage Worriers who are as concerned about AIDS as I think they shld be), but my main reason wld be that I only Fancy V. few people and the chances of them fancying me back are pretty slight so how wld I get the chance to be Promiscuous? I wouldn't want to be Promiscuous with someone I didn't fancy, but maybe that's what Promiscuous people do – just bonk away with anything bonkable, to get practice. Hmmmmm. It wld be V. tiring.

PROSTITUTION

It is hard to see why Prostitutes are so frowned on for selling their bods since Actors and Page Three Gurlz get a high price for what they look like and are Popular Heroes, Heroines, opening fêtes, motor shows Etck. There is always the possibility that you might meet Famous Movie Star Huge Rant, or the Minister of State for Naughty Bits in yr werk, but since this is a family buke, I feel I should point out that although you can certainly buy SEX, you can't buy Lurve. And since SEX and Lurve are V. closely acquainted, paying for it seems a bit misguided to *moi*, though many Boyz (and some Gurlz) look at it differently and say that SEX and Lurve are not the same. Hrrmph.

Sadly, brothels, seedy rooms in Kings X Etck are V. Likely places in which to get an STD (Sexually Transmitted Disease), of which AIDS is one. Also, the Prostitutes are usually at the mercy of vile pimps who start out being nice, giving them roof over head Etck but end up taking most of their earnings and beating them up, so it doesn't look like a V. Good way of earning dosh to *moi*.

It is V. Sad to think of Teenage Worriers, who should be at Dawn of LIFE Etck, ending up doing things they don't enjoy to panting politicians, travelling salesmen Etck because they didn't get any GCSEs, or if they did, they didn't get a job. Even so, most Teen Worriers would rather beg in streets than exchange their vital juices with people they don't fancy. And I am certainly of the latter persuasion.

PSYCHIATRIST

I am also including Therapists here, because they all try to help you when you think your head's going to explode. Most of them look at you with a weird kind of Listening Face. Benjy has a Teddy that looks like this, with its head on one side and

**Wld this be my fate if I slouched to the couch?
And if so, could I tell?**

an expression like someone trying to smile with a
tummy-ache. The Analyst may have studied
Clement – sorry, Sigmund – Freud (all problems
about whether or not you have a Willy), Carl Jung
(all problems about Collective Unconscious, eg: the
clientele of the Dog and Duck on Saturdays) or
Melanie Klein (all problems about recognizing a
Breast is a part of Whole Person – this is supposed
to be just an Infant Phase, but most Boyz I know
haven't realized this).

It may be better to talk to yr Best Frend than go
to Analysts if you have V. Bad Lurve probs,
because it is V. Hard to get therapy on the NHS

anyway, although the NHS ones are at least trained and some of them are V. Good if you are desperately Unhappy. Actually, I wld really like to go myself, about having to say 'banana' instead of that word about dying that rhymes with 'breath' as I feel it is in danger of becoming more of a phobia than an eccentricity. Turning lights on and off twice and bending down to touch the floor again when I drop something are also beginning to be annoying habits . . . but would an Analyst just start blaming my Only Mother and Wrecking our Relationship, I wonder?

I suppose I'd better wait till I am really desperate – otherwise, what will there be to turn to?

I must muse on these and other things while considering whether Agony Aunts, about whom I was less than kind in my first humble volume, are in fact a cheaper option than Analysts or Therapists. Pouring out your probs is half the battle, they say, in this Cruel Werld. Sometimes, just keeping a diary to pour your heart out into might be enough . . . but if you are V. depressed, or have a frend who is, DO go and get advice.

See also DEPRESSION, PHOBIAS.

CHAPTER TEN
QQQQQQZE AND
RRRRRRZE

Dear Reader,

You will not be surprised to find that Daniel did not come at the appointed hour. Nor at the hour after that. Nor the hour after that either. Arg. Perhaps he saw Adam running down the steps after me – and thought we were still together!

Home, distraught, to find Father in tears, clasping scrunched-up piece of paper in one hand and a half empty bottle of whisky in the other.

Glume! It must be a terrible review of his buke! But no.

It was worse.

He had found a note on the table:

Alice.
I'll pick you up at ten.
Neville.

'She'sh left me. Left USH. Packed her bagsh and flown the nesht. Never to bid goodbye! Left thish note.'

And my Adored Only Father, about whom I have
not always been kind, collapsed in a torrent of grief.

'There'sh only one way out,' he wept.

I phoned the Samaritans in a panic and they
tried to talk to him but he is too tearful to speak,
and in any case had been referring to the other
half of the bottle of whisky. I sit with him all
night, sleeping only fitfully, constantly awoken
by thoughts of my Dear Father, as occasioned by
his regular noisy visits to the loo, caused by the
effects of the bottle of whisky and jamming DIY
lock on the door. How could my Mother leave us
all? Her Only Benjy, too? Without even explaining?
And for some seedy millionaire? How callous!
How materialistic!

How . . . um . . . predictable.

I have ignored my Only Family and forsaken them in pursuit of boyz who Don't Care! I should have seen this coming and talked to my Mother before it got out of hand . . .

Granny Chubb comes to rescue first thing in morning. I do not tell her whole truth as Father begs me not to. I beg HIM not to End It All. He looks somewhat surprised, having been cheered up by his Only Mother making him a cup of tea the texture of treacle and a hot water bottle complete with a little stripy, hand-knitted cover of trains and teddies that she'd kept since he was 7 . . .

Meanwhile, I am on the phone to the Komputer Empire founded by Neville. He has been in Barbados for last 6 months, lies secretary.

'But he's stolen my Mother!' I scream.

The secretary becomes somewhat huffy at this point, declaring the seedy Neville's loyalty to his large family of two ex-wives and one current one, thus confirming my worst fears of his adulterous behaviour.

Ring police to say Only Mother has been kidnapped, but they are deeply uninterested when I let slip about the note.

'Sorry, love, but this sounds like a domestic incident. Your Mother clearly went willingly.'

We will have to get a detective agency to track down the dastardly Neville.

I trail glumily to skule two hours late to find Spiggy back. False alarm re dying granddad (evidently granddads are hardier than aunts), who has perked up a treat. She tells me Daniel proposed last night. I consider showing her his letter to moi, but feel I cannot stoop so low, even with my shoulders. Clearly, he thought I wld do while she was away, but when he heard she was back, he didn't even bother coming to meet me. I do not care any more, only thing that matters is return of Mother, happiness of Father Etck.

Just as I am pondering these Deep and Meaningful events, the skule secretary tells me that a note marked URGENT: ATTENTION L. CHUBB has arrived.

Panic.

My Father! My Mother! Banana! Mayhem! Murder! Tragedy! Betrayal! Spokeshave! Etck.

Trembling, I open it.

Dear Scarlett,

My aunt is very well, thank you. Candice, as far as I know, is in Los Angeles, not that I care. Whoever gave you the idea that I did, was gravely mistaken. I am, however, interested in seeing you if you are interested in seeing me.

I shall wait for you outside the school gates tomorrow morning at eight o'clock. This will give you a chance to think things over. I have no desire to force unwanted attentions on you, but I was under the impression (silly me, perhaps) that we were on the verge of something rather special.

Yours,
Adam

THE TEENAGE WORRIER'S GUIDE TO LIFE

*What an amazing note. So sensitive. So caring.
So UNlike Daniel Hope's puke-making, yeechy,
grovelling, Frills & Swoon type phrases.*

*How foolish I had been . . . How could I risk
the affections of one so serious, honest and true for
a fickle fule like Daniel Hopeless?*

*Another ghastly night beckons with its scaly,
rabid claws of Insomnia . . . comforting Father
and Benjy while waiting to hear from appalling
Only Mother. Pretend to Benjy she had to go
away for a couple of nights. If only it were true.
How could she do it????! How will we ever
find her??*

*Father, however, in somewhat better spirits as
Granny Chubb now cosily installed and making
us all boiled eggs with soldiers – including Father,
who says he has not had same since he was boy.*

*Search Yellow Pages for Private Detective
Agencies in vain. Sit weeping by phone. Surely
Only Mother will ring . . .*

QUALIFICATIONS

What you need to fulfil LIFE's missions. Once you
have chosen yr career, you need to check out,
blah drone.

See also CAREER, EXAMS, JOBS.

QUARK

What Quarks MIGHT look like magnified 200,000 zillion times. If they weren't hypothetical . .

I always mix up the diff. kinds of Quarks, and end up concluding that fundamental units of matter that make up LIFE, the Yuniverse and Everything akshully consist of cream cheese. This is, however, a different meaning of Quark, and one that maybe doesn't matter so much to a guide to LIFE, though I'm sure those people who don't mind eating meals that smell like old socks, recently occupied loos Etck wld disagree.

259

Quarks are 'subatomic particles', ie; to whit: V. Small Bitz that make all the Stuff in the Werld hold together. Quarks show how Difficult it has got to be a Scientist these days, and maybe why some Scientists are going back to Religion for explanations for Thingz. Because you can't see them, even with V. Powerful microscopes, clever instruments Etck. They're *hypothetical*, ie: worked out by sums Etck. The physicist who figured them out said he chose the title from a werd the writer James Joyce used in his V. Baffling little buke *Finnegans Wake*, something I have *moi*self attempted to read and which I wld have thought cld have been written by Benjy, but I am prepared to believe Cleverer Persons than El Chubb, viz Ashley and even (sometimes) Adored Mother, who says I will appreciate it in time.

RAINY DAY

While away more Rainy Daze by finding writers whose names are anagrams of food: Keats and steak? Proust and sprout? Yeats and yeast? Build an Ark – why not? Especially if it is VERY rainy.

Many happy hours can be whiled away compiling and weeping over these: photos, letters, scrapbooks. Granny Chubb has V. Good albums, a page of which I have reproduced below. In fact, I think I shld consider publishing them in their entirety and

Me & Ron. Clacton.

Dandelion 1954

Dear Mr Chubb,
You're fired
Yours
F. Atcat

Letter from Ron's
boss.

My first
teabag.

make fortune Etck. That old *Country Diary of an Edwardian Lady* did V. Well, although it is less sure that the *Urban Jottings of an Elizabethan Charlady* has quite the same ring.

See also SENTIMENTAL JOURNEY.

RAVES

Divides Teenage Worriers, because Gurlz usually start dancing younger and do it better than Boyz, though much dancing at Raves Etck does not require fancy footwork but demented flailing about as if with massive electric charge up Beumb. This kind of dancing suits El Chubb because requiring Zilch Expertise, but if you're going to do it you're supposed to do it for a long time without getting tired, which is not easy.

See also DANCE.

REBELS

These are the Yoof you read about. The ones who stay out late, sniffing glue, snorting coke, having orgies Etck Etck. You spend a lot of time thinking: 'When will my mother let me do that?' This means you are not a rebel.

RECYCLING

See ENVIRONMENT.

RELIGION

Sometimes when I see Benjy in hysterics about the floor I think that if he believed in a God who was a cross between Father Christmas and Batman he

**Many Teenage Worriers still have an image
of God like above . . .**

Benjy's version . . .

would Know No Fear. I have V. Mixed Feelings
about godz, and though I think I prob believe in
some kind of Superior Being I am not sure that
the one Granny Chubb believes in is quite the one
for me, though He/She/It seems to have made her
very Contented.

Maybe it's the Christian one being called 'God the Father' Etck that causes the prob, because that makes me think of my Adored Father, and much as I care about him, imagining God like that makes me think of a Big Bearded Man with the Angel Gabriel on his right hand and a can of lager in his left, arguing in V. Deep Old Testament Charlton Heston-type voices about the access code for *CITYSCAPE*.

I think I will need a diff. kind of God, or a diff. kind of religion – possibly like the Buddhist one, which is Somewhat Worryingly based on the inevitability of Yuman suffering, glume, despond Etck. Buddha (it means 'enlightened one') taught that whatever you Desire is changing all the time and so are you, so Desiring things is bound to make you Unhappy. You have to search, therefore, for something beyond the comings and goings of Yuman LIFE, ie, to whit, viz: Enlightenment.

El Chubb's two-watt brain has concluded that the Buddha thought LIFE isn't something fixed like *being*, but a moving stream of *becoming*. Nothing is for ever, so wanting masses of dosh, power over people, facelifts, fame Etck are meaningless. The only thing worth becoming is Truely Enlightened, which is, I suppose, like being in Heaven. I'm not sure I could cope yet with all the sacrifices this Way of LIFE seems to involve (though if you take it seriously enough I suppose they don't seem like sacrifices), and the position of Buddhist teaching on Fudge is V. Difficult to establish, but it's a

V. Interesting antidote to all materialism, interfering
with Nachur Etck.

Islam is a huge and V. Influential religion in
certain parts of the Arab, African and Eastern
Werld. Along with Judaism and Christianity, it is a
'monotheistic' religion, ie: one all-powerful God.
It started in the Arab world in the 7th Century,
and in Arabic Islam means 'surrender'. Allah, the
Islamic God, is all-powerful for Muslims, so the
idea is to surrender to Allah's will. If you are a
Muslim, you will have to face Mecca and pray 5
times a day, fast on the 9th month of the Muslim
year (Ramadan), avoid alcohol, gambling and
lending money for profit (usury). Praying 5 times
a day is no prob for a Teenage Worrier such as *moi*;
I think Adored Father wld definitely benefit from
Muslim teachings on alcohol and gambling; and
lending money for profit is certainly no prob for
Ali El Chubb since I never have any; but some
forms of Islam do not have a great record on their
attitude to us Gurlz, which I have to say puts *moi*
off – although I have to admit that none of the
other religions have been much better in the past.

In general, I don't much care for bossy godz
who demand big personal sacrifices from people
too young, poor or confused to know better. But
some kind of god in yr LIFE can be good for
Worriers, and some people with V. Strong Beliefs
do seem to Worry less, even about V. Big Worries
like Banana. Naturally, fundamentalists of any sort
are political lunies, not religious in the true sense.

REWARDS

MAJOR LIFE-TIP: Reward yrself at every
opportunity. You got dressed? You went to skule?
You spent whole hour without whingeing? You
deserve a reward! Choose from LIFE's rich tapestry
of fun: fudge (nosh of all kinds), bubble baths,
a bunch of flowers, CDs, bukes, frenz' nights
out . . . whatever.

ROMEO

V. Good name for famed Teenage Lurver.
Naturally, because written by an Adult (although
admittedly the V. talented, and not, as far as we
know, gay, W. Spokeshave) Young Lurve goes
badly wrong and we are all supposed to learn a
lesson about burying our differences (which is
better than burying our Teenagers).

ROOMS

The Teenage Worrier's Ideal bedroom is Kool:
spacious, uncluttered, tastefully equipped with
hi-tech modems that zap you into the Internet and
with no hint of a younger or older sibling, or indeed
your younger self. You will have seen this room in
a magazine. There are no visible clothes, because
they have all been packed away into a hi-tech super
storage unit from *Adobe Style* (£490). The sound
system will be minuscule in size but gigantic
decibel-wise (*Adobe Sounds* £596.99). The walls
will be snow-white (*Adobe Tints* £7.50 a can) with
a section reserved for graffiti which will include
the signatures of all your mates plus witty and
pithy comments by yourself about the Nachur of
the Yuniverse, best band, Etck. The elegant futon-
style bed (*Adobe Furnishings* £306) is covered in a

Dream Room Accessories

Versatile drinks dispenser

PC with internet/CD plus video link to Brad Pitbull's bedroom and next year's GCSE papers + answers.

Magic 6" Pegasus that grows when sprinkled with EAU de CARROT and takes me flying at Midnight. (Eat your heart out, Sigmund Freud).

BABE: The magic Piggy-bank that's always full of tenners.

Automatic sock-sorter

Fold-away FACE
with night-time Acne
-banish mode

water bed
with seahorses

Arg. Have just discovered this
is unsound as seahorses are
threatened species. Benjy has
suggested jelly fish.

Neva-Kool: The eternally
hot water bottle.

sumptuous yet understated duvet (*Adobe Fabrics* £37.60). The huge, Manhattan loft-style windows will be covered by venetian blinds (*Adobe Glasshouse* £245.99). The lighting, operated by dimmer switches, (*Adobe Illuminations* £209.76) will individually gleam on those items which express the Individual You. They include: silk screen print by classy photographer of urban wastescape (*Adobe Printshop* £78.90 including clip frame), bonsai tree (*Adobe Orientale* £36) and a designer soft toy of vast but charmless dimensions (*Adobe Care* £39.99) to show you have soft heart.

You've clocked this room in the mag.

If you're smart, you will also have clocked the two-page advertisement for ADOBE – FOR THOSE WHO WANT TO TURN THEIR HABITAT INTO A *NEST, which runs a few pages after the 'objective' feature on the Teenage Room.

* and if this is a nest, I'm an aardvark.

The Teenage Worrier's Real Room is like this:

Marginally larger than the bed in the *Adobe Room* above. It has sky-blue walls with nursery rhyme freeze. Bunk beds – one of which is prob still occupied by 10-year-old sibling. Dark-brown pre-war clothes cupboard that you used to knock on the back of hoping Aslan would leap out and whisk you off to Narnia. The doors do not close and it is overflowing with stuff, only a small proportion of which is still wearable. Floor hazards include: plasticine ingrained irretrievably in carpet; rogue roller-skate; innumerable unidentifiable bits of plastic and fluff; socks without partners; pens and pen tops ditto; gerbil poo; myriad UFOs (unidentified fallen objects). Yr attempts to cover nursery rhyme frieze with posters are charming but without obvious merit either in terms of artistic or interllekshual content – in addition to which, they are crooked. There is a bare light bulb hanging from the centre of the ceiling as you couldn't stand the Winnie-the-Pooh lampshade any more and ripped it out in a frenzy. Yr parents could not or would not afford a replacement. Yr duvet cover is off-white as you have turned it pattern-side down (the pattern being dinosaurs). The curtains are lurid and flowery, having come from some old aunt's lair (yr parents never bothered to buy pretty ones for your room even when you were a baba) but since window is tiny at least there isn't much curtain on view. Sadly, they do have frilly pelmet. Yr attempts to dismantle this only resulted in frayed pelmet.

The only bit of yr room comparable with the *Adobe* one is graffiti corner, where your sibling has drawn a lot of pictures and rude words like 'poo-bum' and 'fart-willy' in indelible marker. The small corner of this midden you can call yr own is shelf above yr bunk bed. On it are: mugs encrusted with green fur; pony books; horror books that you hide the covers of as you don't want to wake up in middle of night with ghouls looking at you (also because they have 'banana' werds in titles); ancient eyeless teddy, ditto elephant, ditto monkey, ditto pink blob; wobbly pile of comics; stack of oddments.

Oddments gather in most corners of most houses except those of pathologically tidy. They include: paperclips, drawing pins, conkers, fluff, dried-up brushes, bits of sellotape, stickers, batteries, tiny bits of felt, dried-up chewing gum, mysterious keys, tissues, thread, buttons, teaspoons, V. Small bottles . . . (*make yr own list here . . .*)

You compare yr lack of room with the style magazine's surfeit of room. And you . . . prefer yr own.

It's cosy. If only it were tidy . . .

TIDYING TIP:

Do it tomorrow.

When tomorrow comes, put everything except duvet and pillow under your bed.

Fish out as necessary.

NB: If you can be bothered, put duvet and pillow on yr bed.

ADOBE room. MY room.

Spot the difference. N.B. pictures drawn at nighttime.

CHAPTER ELEVEN
SSSSSSSSES

*Decide to attempt to drown own sorrows by
looking at my film noire of Urban Glume . . .
Ghastly whining sounds from camera convince me
I have overrun film already, but after usual cursing
and cranking of wrong buttons, levers Etck am able
to replay what the camera has 'seen' from my
window. Glume deepens at realization that one
fixed camera filming for two mins each day is V.V.
Unsatisfactory way of capturing cutting-edge dekay:*

First two mins: *Pavement.*
Second two mins: *Boy (NOT sufficiently
urchin-like, alas, as well washed and akshully in
skule uniform!!!!) playing hopscotch.*
Third two mins: *Rather nice-looking dog
(on lead! Grr!) NOT doing a poo. Followed by
postman wheeling bike and WHISTLING.
(How could he DO that in face of wicked Govt's
decimation of his future Etck.) Sudden fear he may
be postman Aggy's mother ran off with, assuaged
by realization they are abroad . . .*
Fourth two mins: *Plump gurgling baby in buggy
pushed by cheerful-looking parents (TWO of them!*

*One male! One female!); more pavement; a girl in
a flowery frock skipping, with an* ice cream cone.

ARGH! What has
happened to my
VISIONE?

ARGH. What has happened to my Visione?
*My street looks like some perfect place from the
1950s . . . dogs on leads, jolly whistling postmen,
hopscotch, skipping, married couples with babies!!
Am just about to tear up film in despair (while
secretly wondering whether LIFE really does go on
as Normally as this and I only see the Worst Side
because I am a Teenage Worrier . . .) when my
heart leaps up at the sight of the*
Fifth two mins: *a cruising car containing a seedy-
looking punter obviously looking for a hooker. The
door . . . opens . . . a woman gets in . . . Street life
at last!*
But wait.
I am frozen in horror.

I recognize those red high heels.
My Mother.

Dear Reader,
Do not faint (although I nearly did). My Mother
has not (I hope) gone on the streets to sell her
body. She is obviously getting into Neville's car!
I have video evidence! We will be able to trace
the car and save her from a Fate worse than
Banana . . .

Father and Granny Chubb are dipping their soldiers
into boiled eggs and leafing lovingly through snaps
of Dad on a Donkey aged 5 as I hurtle in waving
the camera about wildly. Using Granny Chubb's
powerful magnifying device we decipher number
plate of the Neville-Mobile, and Father, replete
with nursery food, rather relaxedly dials the cops.
I stop him, saying they will not follow up a woman
going off with her fancy man, they have enough to
do with chasing yobs in joy-riding escapades
pretending they are Beverly Hills style cops Etck or
comforting little old ladies with dachshunds stuck
under their baths . . .
But Only Father is smarter than I thought. He
pretends Mother has been abducted. He got number
of car. Urgent they trace it Etck. It seems to werk.
They will get onto it straight away, they say.
Should have news of Mother V. Soon. I thought I
heard my Father murmur 'No rush' but I must
have been mistaken.

*Benjy to bed with Granny Chubb, so sleep a
little better, accompanied by fragment of Hope . . .*

*Perhaps all will be well . . . my Mother home
and, though I struggle to suppress the selfish gene,
my bosom (well, sort of) swells (prinks?) at
prospect of reunion with Adam . . .*

SCHOOL

A lot of rubbish is talked about Skules in the
opinion of *moi*, particularly nowadaze when Govts
are concluding that they don't akshully know why
half the things in the Werld happen, despite all the
posh edukashons of Ministers, Civil Servants Etck,
and now they're trying to make out that if it wasn't
for luny teachers in denims letting children run
around in woad Etck, it wldn't have got like this.

Skules are many different things, because there
are many different kinds of pupils, viz: you and
moi for a start. If you wanted to be V. Meen about
Skules, you might just say they were places to keep
children out of the way of their parents, so Govts
built jails for Yoof called Skules and tortured
them with Lessons. It is prob true to say that most
of what children learn about Reading, Writing
and Maths before they become Teenage Worriers
cld be taught to them V. Intensively in about a year
and the rest of the time they cld spend playing

conkers, Doctors and Nurses, hiding in skips Etck.

But we all know that loads of Skule is V. Boring, so I've tried V. Hard to think of some positive, LIFE-affirming bits about Skule, and I *think* I've succeeded.

Although Skules are partly just ways of solving the prob of where to put children now they can't be sent up chimneys any more Etck, good teachers can be an inspiration, espesh if they believe in making you think hard about thingz you don't normally think about, instead of packing you full of unrelated facts you don't understand. For children living in V. Rough housing, a good Skule can be the most welcoming place they go to, or it wld be if Govts didn't keep encouraging people in nice housing to send their nice children somewhere else, and let the Skules in rough districts get worse. For that matter, a good local Skule can also be the best way to

show V. Privileged Children about Ways of LIFE
quite diff to theirs. Frinstance, at Hazel's posh Gurlz'
Academy they all get given Porsches Etck on their
17th birthday, but it doesn't stop them from putting
slugs in her tennis shoes 'cos she's Gay. And at Daniel
Hope's Skule they think a high-rise is something
their pater (Latin for Dad) gives the chauffeur, but
the bullying goes on even werse than at Sluggs. Also,
there are loads of Druggies at posh Skules 'cos they
have lots more money to chuck around.

I wldn't say Sluggs' Comp is likely to turn out
an above-average number of Nobel Prizewinners or
anything, but it is a meeting place for me and all my
frendz in a place that doesn't cost us money just to
sit down and it does make Clever Kids cleverer
without becoming Obnoxious and Not-So-Clever

Kids feel they amount to something. It also has a lot of pretty interesting thingz you can do in lessons and out, and it mixes a lot of different kinds of people. Just the same, I'd rather be out of it and getting on with becoming World Famous film-maker Etck. And if Mr Hesseltine (our head teacher) is reading this, I'm sure he'll hasten my departure V. Kwick.

See also EXAMS.

SCUFFING SHOES ON PAVEMENT

Major LIFE experience of TWs available at a street corner near you. Campaign for 'Scuffing Cheap Trainers on Pavement' division of this group, as it's not what you scuff but the way you scuff it what counts.

SELF HARM

It is a V. Sad fact that many Teenage Worriers commit acts of self-harm, such as cutting or burning themselves. Usually, this is done in private and the Teenage Worrier thinks they are the only person in the world who is doing such things. It is incredibly important, if you are driven to injure yourself, to try to find help from sympathetic people. There are organisations devoted to helping people who self-harm (see Nos at End of buke) and who are very clear about getting rid of the myths surrounding it, like it's 'just attention seeking', or 'it's self-inflicted so its not serious', or 'if you won't see the psychiatrist you can't want to get better'. These organisations will not tell you any of the above, but instead will try to understand your particular needs – so if you or a frend are self-harming, get in touch. You will feel less alone and may be able to begin to unravel the reasons why you self harm, which are obviously different for each individual.

SENTIMENTAL JOURNEY

That is L. Chubb's Romantick way of having a clear-out. You can quite easily spend the whole holidays doing this if you take enough time crying over each item.

But do you REALLY want to hang on to your first Incy-wincey Pony and its bride's bridle? Or books like *Miss Mouse's Marmalade Adventure, Telling the Time with Mr Worm, Ant, Bucket, Crash!,* or *Purple Penguin's Book of Shades?* (Of course you do: I got enthralled by how Miss Mouse extricated all her little mouselets from the gooey marmalade jar, narrowly escaping clutches of evil marmalade cat Etck.)

Other V. Moving items include V. Early drawings that look like bits of wire wool surrounded by nits and say: 'Hapy mOutH's Dai' or 'I LuV yo baddy', but it is upsetting to find them crumpled up under your bed instead of lovingly pressed between the scented pages of your Mother's scrapbook.

And what is this? A birthday card from your first Lurve, who was a curly-haired bruiser of 7 and invited you to his party, where you got over-excited and were sick in his mother's laundry basket . . .

Your intention to create a whole bag full of rubbish is undermined by the affection you feel for the past. A good compromise is to chuck a few of your sibling's favourite toys out instead. This will create the extra room you need at no personal expense. Draw the line at the Teddy he/she actually goes to bed with, if you want to escape with yr LIFE.

SERVANTS

Domestic servants are making a V. Big come-back! Surprise surprise . . . As the 'work-rich-time-poor' people find they have more dosh but less time, so they are employing the 'work-poor-but-time-rich' folk to do their cleaning, baby-sitting, even shopping Etck. Granny Chubb earned her living like this until V. Recently and there is nowt wrong with it except that the gap between Rich and Poor,

Naturally, one would prefer not to use the same kitchen as one's cook. But times are hard.

instead of getting smaller as you wld hope in Civilized Werld, is actually growing. But, as usual, I have a democratic solution . . .

I have personally always fantasized about having a butler ever since falling in love with Batman's butler Alfred while watching Batman Forever with Benjy. Benjy was much too young for it and dreamt that the floor was full of drain-covers made of dirty grey blancmange through which he wld plunge into Penguin's Lair at every step. But can you imagine the joys of lying on yr hammock calling for a couple of strawberry milk shakes and yr Ferrari to be delivered and finding that a slender cove (dressed as a penguin, as it happens) shimmers up to you to grant yr every whim?

Naturally in El Chubb's Equal Society, everyone wld have butlers, even the butlers. How wld this be? I hear you cry. First, everyone gets a turn at being a butler – say for three months. Then they get a butler of their own. Then, after their turn is up, if they want another butler they have to be a butler again and so on . . . Luxury and penury for all!

SEX/SEX EDUCATION

El Chubb has, of course, dealt with this V. Fascinating subject many times in earlier tomes, but since Teenage Worriers, along with everyone else, never tire of reading about it, I make no excuses for including it again; in fact I'd probably have to have a good excuse if I didn't.

I also have to face the fact that my views on SEX are to some extent guesswork at the moment, though I have high hopes of Adam, of course. It is V. Diff to be a Teenage Worrier who has not Done It because any magazine Worried about its circulation now puts 'The SEX Issue' on its cover, tabloid newspapers put SEX stories on the front page and the opening skirmishes of World War Three somewhere in the Sports section, and

generally you feel that if you haven't Done It yet
it's like standing on the street by yourself outside a
party that everybody else seems to have gone to.

El Chubb arms herself against this particular
Worry with the following:

1) SEX is something people lie about more often
than almost anything else (except maybe Dosh), and
espesh Boyz for whom SEX is a big part of their
egos. Gurlz sometimes make their SEX lives up to
make you jealous, or stop you realizing they're just
as confused about it as you are, and Boyz sometimes
make it up to show you (and each other) what a Big
Deal they are, and how much you'd regret it if you
missed their Once In A LIFEtime offer.

2) At the moment SEX is against the law in
Britain if you're under 16. This does not mean a
large policeman disguised as Rover will spring
out from under yr bed and arrest you for nibbling
yr BeLurved's ear, frinstance, but if you are caught
nibbling V. Intimate partz you and your partner
cld be in for some V. Embarrassing questions
from Adults.

3) Even without Worrying about AIDS, SEX itself
is a risky part of LIFE, because if involves V. Strong
(and sometimes Uncontrollable, phew) Emotions.

Personally, I wld hate a big Promising,
Wonderful thing like SEX to ever be a Habit, and
the Risky bit of it seems V. Exciting. However, I am
not sure I know enough about *moi*self to be ready
for qu. that much Excitement yet, but with the
Right Person I feel sure that I cld trust another
Yuman Bean with my emotions.

4) I do not want to get Pregnant, or catch an
STD (Sexually Transmitted Disease) if I Do It with
someone I don't know just for the sake of Doing It.

Having said all that, and having read what various
Clever People have to say about how complicated
SEX is, you don't have to be a Genius to realize that
Nachur has got on with it pretty well for zillions of
years, and so have Yuman Beans or else we wouldn't
all be here and (mostly) still sane. It is now a regular
part of skule LIFE, however, to go in for something
called SEX EDUKASHUN. Skules have been told by
the Govt that they should emphasize Family Values,

Traditional Morality Etck, when they tell Teenage Worriers about SEX, though many skules prefer to treat it as a Health Ishoo (showing Teenage Worriers trembling on brink of SEXuality how to look after their Bods Etck). Since many members (and I used the word advisedly) of the House of Horrors clearly have V. Big probs re Traditional Morality, viz: Sleaze, Bitz on the Side, Money for Questions Etck, I'm not sure they are the right people to be offering this advice, however.

NB: V. Good contraceptive leaflets are available at your doc's. Read thoroughly.

See also PROMISCUITY.

SHOPPING

Teenage Worriers do a lot of this, mainly for clothes and mainly window-shopping due to lack of dosh. Rebels (see REBELS above) do shop-lifting but L. Chubb does not recommend due to

a) Terror.
b) Guilt.

Shopping for presents is the one kind you have to do at least once a year. If you have a family it gets to be about four times a year. Add frendz' birthdays and that's all your money gone without ever getting a thing for yourself. Adults wld not put up with this. CAMPAIGN FOR TEENAGE WORRIERS' SHOPPING ALLOWANCE. Boyz have an easy time with prezzies as they can get away with a mouldy old bunch of flowers or a cheapo box of chocs and everyone will think they are V. Nice, Trustworthy Etck for bothering at all. Gurlz have to spend hours thinking about what people would actually LIKE. Maybe we shld all just stick to fudge 'n' flowers. V. Easy.

PRESENT-SHOPPING TIPS:
(Have revised these in accordance with new Insight above)
Parents: Fudge
Siblings: Fudge
Frendz: Fudge
Aunts Etck: Flowers.
(NB: Can substitute chocs Etck for fudge if you prefer, as you will note that edibles are given to those you see most of and therefore can be consumed by yourself.)

SIGHTSEEING

V. Good way to find out about LIFE's rich tapestry is to delve into the Past. It is poss to see quite a lot of monuments, sights Etck for free, espesh if you are a good walker and live in London. Skules are sometimes V. Good at organizing trips to places like this, and you should encourage yr teachers to consider it. Remember they need to be told it's for improvement of Yr Mind Etck, rather than opportunity to get off lessons, fiddle about with Darren or Sharon in the back seat of coach Etck.

SKIN

Normal Teenage Worrier's Skin → zit → oily patch ← pluke ← Dry patch

Skin is V. Extraordinary Stuff. It is, of course, just as well we have it, or we wld all have to go round as Skellingtons, which wld not be anything like as nice as the arrangements we have now, though praps if we were all like that it wouldn't matter.

Teenage Worriers do a lot of their Worrying about Skin, espesh whether it's too greasy, too spotty Etck Etck. There are zillions of Skin preparations we spend our meagre quantities of loot on, in the hope they will make us look more like Supermodels, Hollywood stars or Hazel (gnash). But the cheapest and best methods we cld find for looking after our Skin just come down to eating fruit, drinking water, avoiding chocs (shame and not definite evidence about any of this anyway, grrrr), not smoking, and not spending so much of our lives indoors in centrally heated skules, homes, glumey klubs Etck that our Skin never finds out what fresh air akshully is.

This is the sort of Good Advice that Teenage Worriers, including *moi*, find pretty hard to follow, and that's V. Good News for the cosmetics business, which gets people to part with vast fortunes for thingz they cld take care of themselves.

The colour of people's Skins has caused a lot of trouble, and when you come to consider that the reason someone is black, white, olive-coloured or whatever is just to do with how much of this pigment or that is in the epidermis, or outer layer, it doesn't seem like a big enough difference to account for all the fuss there's been over it. Pigments are there as sunscreens, and the only reason for the different-coloured pigments is what kind of exposure to the sun y're likely to get, which is why people from hot countries are darker. And that's all.

Underneath that is the dermis, which is packed with all kinds of interesting Stuff (except that if you can see how interesting it all is, you prob need to get to a hospital fast), including blood vessels, muscles, nerves, sweat glands and the little tubes that keep yr hair on. If the nerves in Yr Skin were not sensitive to heat, cold, pain Etck, Yuman Beans wld be much stoopider than they already are, and spend all their time cutting themselves, getting burnt Etck. All in all, we can pass a hearty vote of thanks for Skin, sez El Chubb. Thank you, Skin.

Normal Teenage Worrier's Skin cont:
Flakey patch   Red Patch   Cold sore   GREASE
(all on a fine layer of PUSTULES)

SPORT

Yes! She's coming up on the inside! She's going faster and higher than any of the other competitors . . . and . . . here it comes! It MUST be the biggest! Let's just see whether the weighing and measuring team will confirm our assessment. They have! It's a Gold for the UK! Letty Chubb has won the First Olympic Nose-picking competition with the biggest, fattest bogey the werld has ever seen . . .

I dread to think what the drugs rools wld be for this kind of competition. Can you put steroids into bogeys?

Many of you have turned the page in disgust, but I draw attention to my only chance of winning an Olympic medal for the following reason: although many of our Sporty types often dream of Olympic wins, they have V. Little chance of achieving this aim in these islands, as Sports facilities in Brit skules are V. Poor and teachers are now so overworked by National Curriculum Etck, that they are unlikely to give up their Saturdays like they used to, to whip their lanky, knobbly, stubby, unwilling adolescents into vibrant teams of fresh-faced energy.

However, Sport is prob more popular now than it has ever been, prob because there is so much of it on TV. Yoof who can't find a job want something that gives them Respeck if they can't get Dosh so they Work Out Etck, and it seems like a quick way to get V. Famous if you practice enough to be

Stand up: the ratfink who invented the PE kit

V. Good at it. Gurlz are also getting into Sports that previously used only to be done by Boyz, including Football. El Chubb thinks that, though Sport can be V. Competitive and Aggressive, it brings Teenage Worriers together and allows you to meet and have fun with people you hardly know or might not otherwise meet. It is also V. Good for the skin, muscles, fitness Etck. It used to be popular with Grown Ups as something that wld stop Teenagers thinking about SEX, but I reckon with all those gleaming muscles, tight shorts Etck on *Match of the Day* the opposite is usually true.

Anyway, Teenage Worriers Unite, campaign for better Sports in skule!

See also EXERCISE, FOOTBALL.

SPOT-SCRUTINIZING

Essential items for this LIFE activity are:

1) Spots
2) Mirror.

Many tragick hours can be whiled away on this LIFE-extinguishing activity. If I counted the hours I have spent bemoaning cratered mug and think how many novels, paintings Etck I might have created, or useful service to the community I might have

If your skin is this bad, you can always look on the bright side and play join the dots

performed . . . But such maundering only leads to more glume and more glume leads to more feverish Spot-Scrutinizing. This is what is meant, I think, by a Vicious Circle.

L. CHUBB'S SPOT TIPS:

1) Do not squeeze them. This advice is impossible to follow unless you wear
   a) A straitjacket
   b) Concrete mittens.
So, if you must, only squeeze the blackheads.

2) Wash face twice a day with antiseptic soap.

3) If they go on and on and on, see doc. Ask about Chinese herbs. Do not despair. 70% of Teenagers get Spots. They will go eventually.

4) Instead of scrutinizing yr own Spots, try scrutinizing other people's. Obviously do this in subtle, caring way, else they will be V. Hurt – eg: take sneaky look, pretending you are admiring shape of their mouth or hooter. NB: Do not assume that if anyone is observing shape of yr mouth or hooter that they are necessarily counting yr Spots.

5) Consider changing breed from 'Person' to 'Dalmatian'.

6) Wear balaclava.

SURGERY

Cosmetic surgery is now another Worry for
Manhattan Babes with loadsadosh. Luckily it is not
a Worry *moi* can afford to have and it's one
American obsession I really hope stays the other
side of Atlantic as far as Teenagers are concerned.
We have enough on plate Etck. It's all done by
stretching and cutting yr skin yeeeech or implanting
collagen (cow fat) or botox. There is no long-term
research on this and no long-term improvements,
either (about 6 months before you need new
collagen or botox – arg). People think they can get
rid of fat by eating loads and having liposuction.
This hoovers your fat off (V. Painful, they say) but
where does the fat go? It sneaks off to gather
elsewhere like yr forehead or something. Silicone's
for bazooms (you WANT a foreign body in you?
Only if he's V. Handsome). And some surgeons are
offering to make Asian people look European by
offering double eyelids! Per-LEASE.

See APPEARANCES and IMAGE.

Plastic Surgeon

ROMAN
NOSES
a speciality

SUPERMODEL
(daft word for model)

Gurlz often want to be models. Clearly this is an unrealistic aim.

Why? 'Cos you have to be a beanpole. If you are short or plump or have anything normal about you at all (like normally squashy nose, normally crooked teeth, mouth, eyes, Etck) you have no chance. Only abnormal Gurlz are models. And they then have to work V. Hard to stay abnormal. 6 hours in the gym and dangerous starvation are part of this 'regime'.

Still, *Yoo-Hoo!*, *Weenybop*, *Smirk* Etc pander to this notion by running competitions for 'Hopefuls' who then starve themselves, iron their wigs, get plastic surgery Etck, in order to earn a fortune.

BE WARNED: if you think it would be fun being a clothes horse who's forced to do exactly what a horde of overpaid photographers and underpaid make-up Gurlz and overpaid fashion editors tell her, then fine. One of you may end up rich, if you are abnormal enough. Also bear in mind that if you *are* V. Byootiful, then you don't need to try to become a Supermodel just to get people to notice you Etck; they will do that anyway (snivel, jealous rage Etck). If you *want* to be a model more than anything else in the werld, that's different.

BUT do avoid ads offering you portfolios of photos for a fee. These are either seedy, or a rip-off.

Make sure you only go to V.V. Reputable agency.

SWEAT

Sweat is OK these days, even for Gurlz. It is, of course, V. Nachural function that stops yr Bod overheating like a car with no radiator, but it has usually been considered slightly Dodgy aspect of Yuman LIFE, which is why perlite people called it Perspiration instead, and a whole industry turned up to hide the smell, marks on clothes Etck, as if people didn't really sweat at all.

With the return of much interest in Body Culchur, werking out, muscle-building (for both Boyz and Gurlz) Etck, Sweat as rather attractive steamy sheen on polished Bods has become OK. It only smells if you don't wash it off every day, or don't wash it out of yr clothes. Teenage Worriers, who often think laundry is something Adored Parents or other slaves are there to do, sometimes ignore these things if Adored Parents, slaves Etck rebel or forget and don't do it. Then you begin to be aware of people moving away from you to other side of room Etck. This is not a good way to make new frendz, espesh of Opposite SEX (Boyz all together often don't seem to notice it, or maybe even enjoy it as macho ritual), so bear it in mind.

CHAPTER TWELVE
TTTTTTTTEEEEEEZE
TO WWWWWWZ

First thing a.m. police say they have traced car to address in Suffolk and are calling round today.

Joy unconfined.

Race to meet Adam before skule.

He is not at skule gates, but wait patiently for an hour and less patiently for a further hour and V. Tragickly for a further hour. In pouring rain. Do not have heart to go to skule two hours late again. Must be some explanation. Must get home to see if any news of Only Mother, anyway.

Arrive home to find it surprisingly cheerful. Granny Chubb, kettle Etck singing merrily in grate, and a gleaming sheen of tidiness suffusing each surface with a well-scrubbed, welcoming glow. Had not realized true colour of kitchen floor till now. Not greyish-green after all, but rather pleasant honey tone.

Police arrived at Suffolk house to find woman answering description of Only Mother who shiftily refused to confirm same and said they couldn't come in without a warrant.

I can't believe it. We have found her (thanks to El Chubb, super-sleuth) and she doesn't want to be found! Not even a word of comfort for her Only Children!

My despair is deepened by the following note which Granny Chubb had propped beside my pillow. It had arrived this morning just after I left.

Dear Scarlett,

I have heard of your affair with Daniel Hope, a person I profoundly despise. Clearly you feel differently and that is your choice. I have decided to take my chance in Los Angeles, where I have been invited to do a Summer Job in Mogul Mogul Junior the Third's studio. Obviously it was a job that held no interest for me while I thought you cared. But now that I know differently, I shall follow my worst instincts and hope to learn the tricks of the trade which I then may use in some way that will help purge the memory of this experience.

As you know, fame and wealth are not on my agenda. But film-making skills are – and I hope to learn them in this environment. I was disappointed to see the use to which you put your beautiful photographs – I had thought better of you.

But I wish you happiness.

By the time you get this, I will be on my way. It is not cowardice that makes me write rather than meet you, but realism.

I know when I'm losing.

Yours,

Adam.

My AFFAIR with Daniel?

Who told him I was even SEEING Daniel? It must have been Aggy! She was the only person who knew! But why would she do such a thing? And what did he mean about my photographs? So many questions remain unanswered but all I know are three Terrible Truths:

1) I have lost Adam because of my stupid faith in Daniel, who has now proved himself beyond the pale for ever.

2) I have been betrayed by Aggy, whom I really trusted.

3) Last and Worst: my parents are splitting up.

This LIFE has become a Vale of Tears, Slough of Despond, Pain Without End Etck. Have written to United Nations asking if I can help out with starving poor, or possibly join Starving Poor as hostage to take my mind off myself.

TANNING

Tanning is becoming unKool owing to skin cancer from sun's rayz. Advice: Wear a Big Hat. Wear good sunglasses so as not to fry your eyes. Wear factor 22. Put it on every two hours or so. But you can take it too far: Ashley went to interview someone

ABOVE: Just a few examples of the SCORN poured on the inventions of Teenage Worriers

CAMPAIGN! For a TEENAGE THINK TANK
to transform LIFE as we know it . . .

of 70 for his skule magazine once. She had stayed indoors for most of her LIFE to avoid sun-ageing. He said she didn't look a day over 69. Sad.

TEETH

All over Werld, Teenage Worriers are gnashing what remains of their Toothy-pegs and remembering tragickly their early visits to dentist, who used to give them balloons and badges for 'star teeth' Etck and who told them to brush twice a day. But did they follow dentist's advice? Did they get that brush up into the corners? Did they use the right brush??? And why – despite endless warblings of 'All I want for Christmas is my two front teeth' – were they rewarded with the crumbly yellow fangs they are currently lumbered with?

Fact is, if you don't look after your Teeth, they will not look after you. But a lot of Tooth Stuff (like so much else in LIFE, sigh_ is hereditary and it's sad but true that some thrice daily brushers are left with krap snappers and vicey versy.

Also, Tooth shape is hardly your fault (though dummies do less harm than thumb-sucking apparently . . . but it's too late for you to think of that now, except for your own offspring). If you need braces, why not colour co-ordinate them with yr socks? All sorts of colours available nowadays.

Don't get too hung up on Teeth. Strong and healthy is better than straight and white and lots of the best faces have quirky fangs. The Americans spend fortunes on their mouths, and so will you if you leave it too late as NHS dentists are fast disappearing. Get stuff fixed early while you're entitled to Free dentistry. After that, grin and bear it (or perhaps that shld be smirk and don't bare them?).

TEXTING

Alas and woe the joy of txt is closed to *moi* until I can get a new mobile. Maybe shld try the joy of sx instead (chance would be a fine thing).

TRAINERS

Museums of the future will be V. Interesting places for footwear. Future folk will ask: Did twenty-first-century BritKids actually wear that stuff? But while Trainers are obv V. Much more sensible Etck than Stilettos, their prices are certainly not. Wot, I ask you, are we paying £90 for? A label? An 'air bubble'? Silver laces? LIGHTS? Per-LEASE. I have, like all Teenage Worriers, done my share of yearning for *Tike Vampires*, complete with retractable

**If beset by Trainer-Worry
why not consider the humble clog?**

Or El Chubb's Jester-Boot (patent pending)

roller-blade, CD player, automatic kick-yer-enemy-
into-next-year function Etck Etck. But I ponder ye
economics and I have regrettably to say there are
better things (fudge, G. Chubb's glasses) on which
to spend the dosh. 'Course, if they invent a pair
with WINGS, then I'll be singing a different toon.
So far, they have only put wings on sanitary towels
and these, as far as I can see, do not need to fly.

Then there's the added Fashion-Worry of LACES.
Yurg. It's bad enuf when you are 7 and have to
change for PE and you are the only child in class
who can't do its laces up and your horrible parent

has forgotten that you begged to wear velcro shoes.

When you are a Teenage Worrier it gets a whole lot worse, as you have to lace 'em horizontally, only using one half of the laces, or lace them top-to-bottom missing out centre holes, or wear the laces just round your ankles. See how fickle changing fashion is? Buy cheapo slip-on plimsolls and avoid this fashion Worry. El Chubb predicts you will start a new Superkool wave.

See FASHION.

=ʒ= TRANSPORT

Getting Around is a Big Prob for Teenage Worriers, due to lack of dosh, inability to drive Etck.
It is usually necessary to call up Adored Parents minicab service, which they particularly dislike when summoned 30 miles to some scuzzy klub in the middle of the night.

If you live in London, tubes are OK and not *too* expensive as long as you get right Travelcards Etck and have big advantage for Geographical Dyslexics like *moi*, in that they TELL YOU WHERE YOU ARE. Why don't bus stops have names on like tube stations? It wld be so much easier. (Thinks: Cld create a bus map like the tube map and make fortune.)

In fact, most Teenage Worriers out late generally

An e.g. of my sympathetic folks?

prefer the buses, which can be qu. nice sociable
places to travel around: there's something to look
at if you end up having seething silent row with
Person you're travelling with; they run later at
night; and they have V. Big advantage of not being
full of looooong echoing corridors empty except
for lurking muggers Etck.

Late travel on public transport, however, is an
opportunity to see the Adult Werld at its worst,
and it is V. Diff to see how the Older Generation
can be qu. so fussy about Terrible Teenage Habitz
when you realize how many of them are staggering
around the city barely able to stand.

If you live in a country district, travel and transport is a V. Big Prob indeed, and you are usually
forced to rely on Adored Parents and Parents'
frendz with cars, which can restrict yr freedom and
sense you are growing up into a proper autonomous

Avoid traffic chaos –
learn to ride a unicycle

Person. But much better to put up with that than
walk alone in deserted districts at night, or try to
hitch lifts. These can turn out in some cases to be
frightening or even dangerous activities, and are
Not Recommended by El Urban-Groover Chubb,
even though she thinks a stile is deciding to wear a
bin-liner with a plastic tiara Etck.

Obviously ye trusty bicycle is V. Imp for most of
us, but El Chubb stresses importance of right safety
gear, fluorescent belts, cycling hats Etck – better to
look nerdish than . . . er, meet the Grim Reaper.
Also, it just isn't safe to cycle in busy cities unless
there's a proper track. Campaign for cyclists'
pavements that are safe as pedestrians' pavements!

TRAVELLERS

Folk-lore will describe the Gypsy thus: Dastardly,
beggarly ne'er-do-wells who steal innocent children.

Also, V. Romantick curly-haired ear-ringed Lurvers who whisk you away to rural idyll. As usual, Opinion-formers take one view, and Teenage Worriers take the other. Truth, inevitably, lies in between. So if yr Gypsy Lurver brings out the Gypsy in yr Soul but the fascist in yr father, take heed. Age and wisdom do count for *something* and it may be that your aged parent discerns a less than worthy soul beneath the glittering surface. (Goodness, is this *moi* speaking? Why am I giving such measured Advice? – Because, dear Reader, I have been Betrayed. And I have seen my Mother Betrayed. And I have seen my Father Betrayed – his Gypsy was Spangly Angy, who ditched him for the snake charmer.)

Real-LIFE Gypsies, of course, are Romany Travellers, who are sadly being routed from our countryside by an Uncaring Govt. These are distinct

Could this be the gypsy in my soul? Swooon . . .

from New Age Travellers, who are just like you and me but prefer a LIFE on the open road. This seems like a V. Good option in today's uncaring werld of shrinking council housing, huge mortgages and huger rents. And, given latest statistics of homeless young people, it seems like that's what most of us are being forced into anyway. I wld rather try to get hold of a small horse and cart and a tent than live on the Strand in a cardboard box . . .

SUPPORT GYPSIES! FREE CAMPING FOR ALL! (this handy two-in-one slogan also to apply to Gay Campaigns).

VEGETARIANISM

Large numbers of V. sensible Caring Teenage Worriers have become Vegetarians of late. Their numbers were doubled by the BSE scare and quadrupled by *Babe*, the V. cute film about a talking piggy which put Benjy off sausages for a whole day. There are some good arguments for and against this: If we didn't raise any sheep or cattle we wouldn't have much grass; it would all be given over to other crops and the countryside wld look V. Different. On the other hand, it is V. Uneconomic for the world to get so much of its protein from meat (soya wld produce more protein more cheaply) and modern methods of factory

farming are extremely cruel and, it now seems, possibly very harmful to ye food chain.

Also if you are still growing, it is V.V.V. Imp to get enough protein, which requires a bit of thought if you are a Vegetarian. Most veggies eat some animal products which do not involve killing animals – ie: eggs, butter, milk, cheese: all V. Good for protein, as are nuts and soya beans. I feel I shld be a Vegetarian, but instead have been perswading Only Mother to buy organic meat and free range chickens. More expensive but at least you know they've had a happy LIFE.

See DIET.

VIDEOS

Last week we became the last family in Little Britain to buy a video recorder. We have been renting for years but it always breaks. So now, when Adored Mother and Father decide they're going to have A Treat (which they do about once every fifty million years) they'll be like everyone else: rent a video and get an Indian takeaway. Except that now everyone is renting DVDs, moan whinge – we are always 3 steps behind. If this is an example to Us Yoof about how to live LIFE to the full, drink deep of the cup of Yuman Experience, climb every mountain, dare to LIVE and dare to

cry Etck, then the sooner those people who keep
saying the World's going to end on Tuesday week
get their way the better.

I'd always rather see the films that I really like in
the cinema, because once you've seen them there
watching them at home is like listening to
Rachmaninov's Third Piano Concerto played on
a xylophone. Videos can, of course, be useful for
watching stuff you're not supposed to. I went
round to Hazel's house one night when her parents
were out and she had a Video called *Wild
Awakening*, which was about a Boy and Gurl
sounding as if they're having asthma attacks
most of the time, and tearing at each other's zips,
buttons Etck on buses, in public loos, behind
bushes, in cars Etck Etck. I was V. Excited by all
this for a bit, but after a while we switched it off
and played Scrabble instead.

I do find Videos are one area of Home LIFE
where us Teenage Worriers can get a bit of control
of the situation. This is because many Adored
Parents can't understand new electronic Video
Machines and tellys and tear up the instructions in
Video Rage Etck, so it's often us who are the only
ones who know how to work it all. Akshully,
having been V. Keen to join herd and get one of
these, I have trouble with it *moi*self, but I leave it
to Benjy who understands it by instinct, and then
pretend it was me.

VIRTUAL REALITY

In case you hadn't noticed, komputer graphics are getting so good these days they almost look like film, and imitation of Reality has become V. Amazing, making screen games Etck much more exciting than they used to be. This has led to the opening of huge Virtual Reality centres and theme parks, where Teenage Worriers are to be found spending a lot of time and dosh careering around Virtual racetracks, down Virtual ski-slopes, through Virtual battlefields Etck.

Development of this technology now goes on so fast that what is Mind-boggling one year is Dead As Dodo the next, and it must be like Christmas every day for the makers of this Stuff, because the Effex are constantly changed and people don't get bored. People grow out of it instead, though in the case of my Adored Father this is not true, and when we all went to Hyperwerld once, he was the one who wouldn't leave.

But El Chubb has to confess to being bored by a lot of this Stuff and when she tried the Virtual ski-slope she had to be led away with panic attacks. Benjy, however, despite the fact the floor was constantly disappearing from under him, loved every minute of it and it might turn out to be V. Good aversion therapy for his phobia, although almost as expensive as hiring a private head-doctor. For *moi*self, I would like to see a Virtual Romance game, where you could give the machine a pic of yr Elusive BeLurved, and it immediately creates a steamy satin-sheets scenario with the Person of Yr Dreamz and you together in it, doing Whatever You Want (pant, sigh, heave Etck). I fear, however, that if this came to pass, you might end up feeling a bit Seedy that the Person wasn't really there to go and have a Strawberry Milkshake with afterwards.

But then maybe if Virtual Reality got that good, they *would* be.

Teenage Worry factor No. 543: How would we then know who was the Real person and who wasn't? Would it matter? Would the Real People just stay at home in a kind of fridge, while Virtual Clones of them went out and Did Thingz? Will this be clutched on to by Werld Govts as way of solving food shortage, crime wave Etck? Answers to Teenage Think Tank please . . .

VOLUNTEERING

Tidy up a boy scout TODAY!

V. Good to do werk for nothing for people who have even less than Teenage Worriers. Our local charity shop was closed for two days before Christmas this year (just when they could be doing really well) because of lack of Volunteers. Yeeeeech, guilt. Two hours a week doing something V. Caring is Good for Soul, sez *moi*. Must make it New Year's Resolution for year 20000.

WALKING

What? El Chubb donning boots made out of bits of Stonehenge and toting horrible rucksack through

mud and brambles in hearty manner? No fear. I prefer a short walk to the chip shop, but we're all different and I do have a sneaky admiration for those V. Energetic healthy types who storm off over hill and dale whistling a happy tune. In Olden Times like the 1950s, it seems people used to think this sort of thing was V. Good for combating the onset of Sekshul Urrrrges in Teenage Worriers, or even for stopping them becoming Worriers at all, because they wld be bursting with Godz Fresh Air, brains pulsating with oxygen, capable of no more at night than falling into a dreamless, fantasyless sleep as soon as they hit the pillow. Reluctantly, I am forced to admit that exercise is prob. V. Good for mental energy, optimism Etck, but personally I wld rather dance, train to become Gladiator, take up karate Etck than clump around the countryside in jumper made from about 50 sheep, with half the contents of my room on my back.

On *le autre main*, walking V. Good for body, soul, environment, and espesh for gurlz' bones, which otherwise crumble with dread osteoporosis. So do those 10,000 steps a day (guilt, lash).

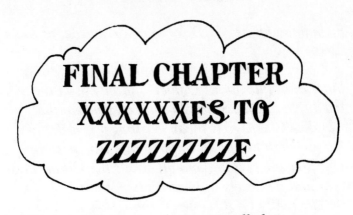

FINAL CHAPTER XXXXXXES TO ZZZZZZZE

Look, I'm glad to say a lot's unravelled since my last chapter – most of it is pretty good and some of it is terrible. The terrible thing was that Sleeve SOLD my photos to the horrible tabloid newspaper the Slob so that Aggy was plastered all over the centre spread as an image of a typical poor, black Londoner. What was worse, they retouched the pics to make it look as if she was surrounded by about a hundred babies, plus nicked tellys, mobile phones Etck and showing her knickers as well.

The paper banged on about how there were too many people like Aggy and they were SPONGING OFF THE WELFARE STATE, causing Tidal Wave of Crime Etck. I couldn't believe it.

Not surprisingly, Aggy had thought it was ME who sold the pictures and had immediately told Adam I was seeing Daniel. I don't blame her, not one bit. I can't even get Sleeve, because he had bought the pictures off me with an 'Option' (which I didn't understand, of course, but now realize means Option to Stitch Up Dumb Artist Etck). But his name will be MUD for ever, or Merde, as the Euros say.

I have written to Adam explaining everything, but I didn't lie about Daniel, and he hasn't written back. He probably has discovered by now that Candice Cleavage (I mean Carthage) is a Better Person than her father (apparently her first film was amazingly good and all about the Urban Poor . . .) and definitely a Better Person than moi.

The really GOOD news, though, is that my Mother was not seeing the ex-student-turned-kom-puter-wizard after all!! 'Neville' was a happily married tutor on the komputer graphics course whose WIFE had invited my Mother over for a few days to discuss starting up a small business! Mother had left a message on the ansaphone about it and had also written Dad a note, viz:

Sweetheart,

Buzzing off for a couple of days to make loads of dosh (I hope) so we can all be comfy again. I'll be staying with Vera Snythe and her husband Neville at (then she gives the Suffolk address). Have left half a sausage roll in fridge. Will ring tonite.

All love.

Unfortunately, my Mother, being in a bit of a tizz, had left Neville's note to her on the table and put her note to Dad in her handbag. Arg. My Father, having the gadget wizardry of a

technically challenged amoeba (as proved by his
only ever getting to level 2 of the kiddies' game
CITYSCAPE, despite pretending otherwise) had
managed to disconnect ansaphone and – after
tearful call to Samaritans – had not put our phone
back on hook properly. Meanwhile police had
called on furious Mrs Snythe (who looks a bit like
Mother), who had no idea what they were talking
about. She only pieced it together when she told
Neville and my Mother about the police coming.
My Mother had enrolled on the course as Ms
Gosling and neglected to mention her relationship
with my Adored Father. This had been my Only
Mother's touching attempt to seem Young(ish) and
Free of Responsibilities and therefore a dashing
business partner for Mrs Snythe. Therefore police
at door going on about missing wife of Leonard
Chubb (which is how my demented Father referred
to her) had naturally meant nothing to poor Mrs
Snythe. When Mother heard about the police she
put two and two together and surged home to find
us all in mourning . . .

Well, not quite. We had by then discovered the
joy of having Granny Chubb making boiled eggs
and soldiers for us all and generally cosseting us
more than we were accustomed to. After an initial
moment of feeling hurt, my Only Mother made a
tentative suggestion. Why didn't Granny Chubb
move in? We could halve all our living expenses
and have boiled eggs, cauliflower cheese and apple
pie every day!

Rover, Benjy, Father and me Over Moon at this suggestion. And so, dear Readers, I am feeling V.V.V. Much better. I have explained ALL to Aggy (who believes me), and have enrolled in another film course as I am going to take my career prospects seriously now. We have divided the front room so Granny Chubb has her own space – shared for much of the time with Darling Father, for whom she is knitting a pair of bedsocks. Sharing space has proved economical and (blush), with a little help from guilt-stricken Only Father, I have finally saved enough in my GCSE fund to buy Granny Chubb a decent pair of specs. It's nice to have one thing to be proud of. Also, does Coming of the Bedsock mean I will be saved from the Invasion of the Boleros? Anyway, it is touching to see how V.V. Happy she is.

My Mother is now let off the domestic hook as G. Chubb does all the catering – and she is making headway with her business! And Dad got a nice review of his buke in the poshest Sunday paper. Which means, according to his publisher, that the others will start, too.

Benjy's floor phobia is in recession (either due to the stunning new cleanliness of said floors or possibly the comforting presence of G. Chubb). Maybe a rosy future beckons after all.

But one thing I have learnt, both from my use of Hazel's video and the SLOB's use of my photographs: sometimes, the camera CAN lie.

L. Chubb's Year

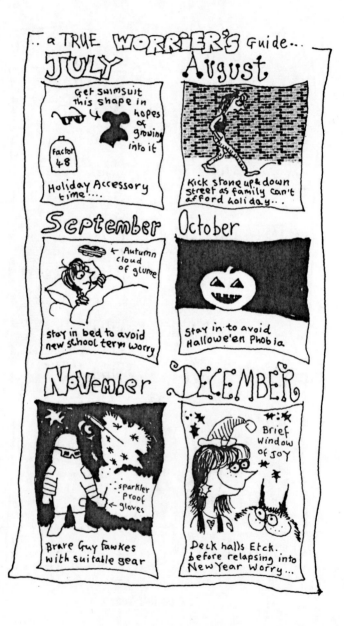

XANADU

Where Kubla Khan decreed an ancient Pleasure Dome, according to ye poet Coleridge. V. Nice, if only he would decree a Pleasure Dome on each mean street inhabited by Teenage Worriers.

YES — Ending on Happy Note dept.

Just say 'Yes' to LIFE, suggests L. Chubb. Explore all possibilities and do not be cowed by glumey cows like *moi* who preach dume. Make a list of all yr major Worries (er, keep a copy . . .). Then screw up list, tear into a thousand tiny pieces and scatter to the wind (I mean put neatly in dustbin liner, to avoid litter-guilt). Your Worries have now disappeared. You can check the copy you kept two or three times a day to make sure you are not Worrying . . .

And after you've done all that, you can forget about ZODIACS, ZEBRAS, ZEUS, ZONES and just snoozzzzzzzzzzze . . .

One of LIFE'S burning questions: "Do fleas sleep?"

FILL IN NOW

If you want to...

Date:

Biggest **WORRIES**:

Biggest **HOPES**:

Best **PEOPLE**:

Best **THINGS**:

OTHER (worries, fears, hopes, dreams, loves, hates....)

PTO →

ONE YEAR LATER

Wait a year (YES! go on!) and then
fill this in (WITHOUT sneaking a look
at the page Before)
Date:

Biggest **WORRIES**:

Biggest **HOPES**:

Best **PEOPLE**:

Best **THINGS**:

OTHER (worries, fears, hopes, dreams,
loves, hates...)

V. Interesting to see if stuff is better,
worse or same. Gives, um, PERSPECTIVE
Etck. (IF WORSE, bound to get better,
cos that's **LIFE**).

by Ros Asquith

The Long-Awaited sequel to the best-selling
I WAS A TEENAGE WORRIER

Yes! Here it is! From moi, Letty Chubb, ages 15.
A thrusting, PASSIONATE, JUICY, (phew, must hurl
self into cold shower) Look at EVERY aspect
of LURVE.

'Hilarious . . . will help with any questions to do with
the L-word' *TV Hits*

'Good for a laugh and great advice' *The Times*

Only £5.99!
0 552 55281 X

HELP!

Useful telephone numbers for serious LIFE worries . . .

CHILDLINE
Freephone 0800 1111
www.childline.org.uk
A confidential free 24-hour phone line if you are in trouble or danger.

THE SAMARITANS
08457 909090
www.samaritans.org.uk
24-hour emergency service for the suicidal or despairing. If in serious trouble, DO CALL.

ALATEEN (part of Al-Anon)
020 7403 0888
(Mon-Fri 10am-4pm)
020 7407 8180
or 020 7407 7878
(Mon-Fri 4pm-10pm;
weekends and bank holidays 10am-10pm)
www.al-anon.alateen.org
Confidential helpline if you are affected by the drinking problem of a family member or friend.

DRINKLINE
Freephone 0800 9178282
(Mon-Thurs 9am-11pm;
Fri-Sun 24 hours)

Confidential, national alcohol helpline. Very helpful with advice on drinking levels Etck. Free information packs.

DEPARTMENT OF HEALTH NATIONAL DRUGS HELPLINE
Freephone 0800 77 66 00
(Everyday 7am-11pm)
A free and confidential service available in a range of languages other than English. Free leaflets and literature.

BROOK ADVISORY CENTRES
0800 018 5023 (Helpline, office hours)
020 7617 8000 (Recorded information helpline)
www.brook.org.uk
Contraceptive and counselling service for the under 25s. Local clinics throughout the UK. Under 16s can obtain confidential help.

NATIONAL SELF HARM NETWORK
NSHN
PO Box 7264
Nottingham
NG1 6WJ
www.nshn.co.uk